"This wasn't a date," Rose pointed out

Her tenacity made Brendan smile. "It can be."

She shook her head with an air of desperation. "No, it can't."

Wanting to change her mind, he tried a more understanding tone. "Why not?"

"Because it shouldn't be. You're just here for this fund-raising campaign, right?"

"Right." He hoped it proved successful. He *needed* it to be successful.

"Then you're going back to New York?"

"So the fact that I don't live in Chicago is the problem?"

She gave a short sarcastic laugh. "Actually, that's the one good thing."

Surprised at how stung he felt, Brendan shifted away from her. "I take it you simply don't want any sort of relationship with me."

"I don't want a relationship with anyone."

It wasn't personal. He could work with that. *Keep it physical.* "Perfect. Neither do I. So let me come home with you."

MacDOUGAL MEETS HIS MATCH

Leah Vale

HARLEQUIN®

TORONTO • NEW YORK • LONDON
AMSTERDAM • PARIS • SYDNEY • HAMBURG
STOCKHOLM • ATHENS • TOKYO • MILAN • MADRID
PRAGUE • WARSAW • BUDAPEST • AUCKLAND

ISBN 0-373-75006-4

MACDOUGAL MEETS HIS MATCH

This edition published by arrangement with Harlequin Books S.A.

® and TM are trademarks of the publisher. Trademarks indicated with ® are registered in the United States Patent and Trademark Office, the Canadian Trade Marks Office and in other countries.

Visit us at www.eHarlequin.com

Printed in U.S.A.

Dear Reader,

Some secondary characters in books just aren't meant to stay secondary, even when their first appearance is only a few lines. Brendan MacDougal turned out to be one of those characters.

The guy barely spoke in *The Rich Girl Goes Wild*, his eldest brother Wilder's story, but he immediately started nagging me for a book of his own. Trust me, a hero like him is hard to turn down. But who to pair with such a charmer, a man capable of talking people out of their money in the name of worthy causes?

Why, a woman with the nickname Dr. Doberman, that's who. Pediatric neurologist Rose Doeber knows something about charity, and not because she was on the donating side. She also knows the price of fame, and is determined to protect the little boy she is trying to adopt from having to pay that price.

But Brendan needs her help. He has to repair the damage done to his family's charity foundation when he trusted a woman who turned out to be a thief. Rose and the little boy are just the ticket to restoring his reputation. Or are they?

I hope you enjoy reading their story as much as I enjoyed writing it.

Leah Vale

To Ross
For all your love and support

Chapter One

"Here. You don't want to soak the little guy."

Rose Doeber blinked hard to make sure she wasn't looking at a late night hallucination. After all, the light in the small, semiprivate hospital room was dim, and tears did tend to blur things. But when she refocused her eyes the big, gorgeous, dark-haired man in a black tuxedo was still standing on the other side of the only occupied railed bed from her, towering over the child asleep in it. He appeared as real as the snow-white handkerchief he was offering her.

Not exactly used to being comforted by incredible-looking men in formal wear, she couldn't think of anything else to do but reach toward him. He quickly rounded the bed, his shiny black shoes noisy on the sterile white linoleum, and gave her the handkerchief.

"Thank you." Her voice came out low and rough, transformed by the tears she'd hastily tried to wipe away when he'd first startled her with some sort of comment about believing laughter was the best medicine.

When he'd first spoken from the shadows near the open door, beyond the reach of the bedside light, Rose had feared she'd been caught by a fellow member of the hospital staff. She was well aware that most of her co-workers thought she was as hard as nails and much older than her thirty-one years. She'd rather drink iodine than let any of them see her too-soft underbelly that her tough and tenacious routine was meant to protect. She'd learned long ago that if no one knew she was vulnerable, no one could hurt her.

Only late at night in the quiet of Chicago General's pediatric ward, the place that had become her universe, did she let her guard down. Only at Dylan's bedside did her worries about her bid to adopt the three-year-old overwhelm her.

And that was when the memories came.

Memories of waking up in this very hospital, a frightened six-year-old, with no idea who she was or why she'd been left unconscious under a rosebush in a city garden. Memories of how no one had come forward to claim her.

That abandonment hadn't been her last, either.

She held the handkerchief to her eyes and clenched her teeth against the familiar pain. She refused to let Dylan start down that road. But with his incarcerated father stalling the adoption process, Rose had finally lost control tonight and succumbed to rare tears.

She'd been so alone for so long, with Dylan the only emotional connection she could trust, that she'd thought her stressed mind had conjured up the image of her perfect man, a tower of strength and reliability. Someone who would never use her or abandon her.

Someone who didn't exist.

The guy in the tux said, ''You're welcome'' and shook her from her self-pitying thoughts.

While he might look like the sort of apparition that a heart as lonely as hers would conjure up, the rasp of his deep voice along her senses felt very real. And there was no denying the spicy, heady scent the fine cloth handkerchief had picked up from its owner. It was a sharp contrast to the disinfectant-tinged hospital air.

He quietly cleared his throat, as if the rough edges of his baritone weren't normal, either. ''Is there anything else I can do for you?'' His voice was much smoother now, almost cultured. ''Call your husband? Boyfriend?''

Rose scoffed as she wiped beneath her eyes with his incredibly soft handkerchief. ''I'm not married. No boyfriend.''

He was silent for a moment, then added, ''Is there anything you need?''

Too drained to throw out her usual response—*to be left alone*—she shook her head and dabbed at her nose. "No."

"Are you sure?" he pressed. "I'm amazingly resourceful."

Dropping her hands to her lap, she looked down at the square of linen he'd pulled from within his tuxedo jacket, the white fabric stark against her black knit pants. Heaven only knew what a resourceful man might have tucked between the white shirt covering his flat stomach and his black cummerbund. She gave a rueful laugh. "I don't doubt that you are, but there's no way you could get me what I need."

"Try me," he countered in a tone that made it clear he felt the need to prove her wrong.

She met his gaze. His eyes appeared light brown in the lamp's dim glow. Probably hazel. Definitely warm with concern.

He raised a dark brow, reminding her that he was waiting to hear what she needed. Whatever he was delusional enough to think he could get her.

Maybe he had reason for his delusions, though. He was clearly a man of means. No rental tux would ever fit the way his did. The set of his square jaw and the studied effortless style of his slightly wavy hair suggested a man who did what he wanted, and did it well.

If only this wedding magazine escapee really *was* her perfect man. Her dream come true.

Yeah, right.

When she remained silent, he reached out and laid an impossibly strong and tanned hand on the beige blanket at the end of the bed, a gold class ring glinting on his right ring finger. He directed his attention to Dylan. "Is he in a bad way?"

Rose followed his gaze, her heart melting as always at the sight of the precious towheaded little boy, his well-loved Bunny held close. "No. Thank God. For the most part he's fine. Some digestive issues, but nothing serious." She touched a gentle hand of her own on the sheet covering Dylan's round tummy. "He just doesn't speak. We're trying to figure out why."

She completely understood Dylan's inability to talk, just as she had finally come to understand—and accept—her inability to remember why she'd been abandoned. Some things were best left unsaid or forgotten. That was what made her and Dylan kindred souls.

Even though she knew what demons inhabited his nightmares along with his vital statistics, she still thought of him as her Little Mr. Nobody, just as she'd thought of herself as Little Miss Nobody while growing up. No one had wanted her, and no one wanted him.

No one but her.

The man asked, "How old is he?"

"Three. He's small for his age. But tough. So very tough." The police had found him in a nest he'd made in the closet for himself and Bunny. While he never made a sound, he was quick with his sweet smile.

"There must still be some way I can help."

She gave a soft, wry laugh. "You wouldn't happen to be a family court judge, would you?"

"No, but I occasionally play golf with—"

She waved him off. "That's okay. Really." She eyed him again. "You look like you have more important plans for the night than helping me out."

He squatted next to her. The light from the bedside lamp glinted off his hair, which turned out to be the richest mahogany color she'd ever seen. The richest and most touchable. With him so low and less imposing, so close and smelling so good, it was harder for her not to meet his eyes.

A small smile curled the edges of his sensuous mouth, and something tightened in her belly. "If I can give you a reason to smile, then there's nothing more important I could be doing."

His canned charm made Rose smile despite herself. The flare of appreciation in his eyes jolted her with self-consciousness. She resisted the urge to smooth her hair—or his—and shifted her attention back to the white handkerchief she was gripping with both hands in her lap. Heat still flushed her cheeks. He really *had* caught her in a weak moment. The temptation to go with the fantasy of him being her dream man was overwhelming.

His deep voice, inexplicably soft and now dangerously smooth, breached her ancient defenses even more. "Did something happen that might cost you custody of your son?"

Laughing hollowly at how close he'd come to the truth, she shook her head. "That's just it—he's not my son." The words burned her throat.

From the moment they'd called her in to assess Dylan for possible neurological damage from his deceased mother's drug use or, God forbid, physical abuse, Rose had fallen in love with the little boy. And she wanted nothing more than to be the mother he deserved.

"Not yours? Really?" The man stood and looked from her to the sleeping child. "He sure has your coloring. The same blond hair, fair skin, fine features. What is he to you?"

Her fantasy man's pointed questions were just what she needed to slap her back to reality. A reality that set off alarms in her head.

She murmured her usual farewell to Dylan, "Love you," then stood and retrieved her white lab coat from the back of her chair. She pulled it on over her blue cotton shirt as she placed herself between the man and Dylan. "I'm sorry, but what exactly is your business here at the hospital so late?"

She made a just as pointed perusal of his tuxedo. "Visiting hours were over some time ago."

He eyed her in turn, clearly noting her identification badge and the card key hanging from a long, shoe-lace type cord covered with bright yellow smiley faces.

He nodded and mouthed a silent *ah.* "I'm here scouting the hospital for photo ops for my race-car-driver brother. We're doing a safety promotion campaign to raise funds for the expansion of the pediatric wing."

He looked back at the bed and its occupant. "You know—" he inclined his head toward Dylan "—this little guy would be perfect to pose with Rory. Especially since his health isn't as delicate as some. If this warm spring weather holds, we could even use him in the outdoor shots. Do you think his parents would go for it?"

Cold panic seized Rose by the throat, closing off her airway with its icy grip. What if Bobby Ray saw his son with someone famous on the news, or on some commercial? Though Folsom Prison was a long way away in California, Bobby Ray might think he could benefit somehow, and change his mind about allowing her adoption of Dylan to begin.

She couldn't bear the loss, and Dylan didn't deserve the abandonment.

She shook her head sharply. "No. Not Dylan."

The man's eyebrows shot up.

"As the attending pediatric neurologist on this case, I can't allow it. Now if you'll step into the hall…" She held out a rigid hand toward the door.

He complied and started to leave, but didn't take his surprised gaze from her. "Pediatric neurologist. Hmm."

She herded him back out into the hall, dimly lit in deference to the children who couldn't sleep behind a closed door. Like so many of these kids, Dylan was additionally burdened with a fear of the dark.

Delores, the head night-shift nurse, was double-checking a tray of pills on a cart across the hall. She raised her gray brows at the man in the tux, who nodded a greeting and winked at her. She grinned in a way that took thirty years off her kind, wrinkled face.

No wonder he'd looked so stunned when Rose had told him no. A man as sexy and charming as him probably had never heard the word before.

Delores returned to what she'd been doing, selecting a cup of meds, then disappeared into the room opposite them. As soon as she was gone the man lifted a hand, his onyx cuff link flashing ominously, and pointed at Dylan. "He'd really get a kick out of my brother Rory. He's great with the kids."

Rose crossed her arms and raised herself to her full height, which at 5'9" was usually more than enough to be imposing, but she max'ed out at this guy's slightly cleft chin. Not exactly equal footing.

To pretend she hadn't noticed, she raised her own chin a notch. "No. Dylan is off-limits. Now, if you'll excuse me…" She uncrossed her arms and stepped around him. When he didn't move, she gestured in the direction opposite to where she intended to go. "You'll find the most direct way out down that hall."

He raised his hand in acknowledgment, but didn't leave. He just continued to watch her, his expression assessing, probing, chipping away at the facade he'd already had a peek behind. He'd tempted her once to shift her burdens to his broad shoulders, but she wouldn't. He wanted something she couldn't give.

While Rose knew she should stick around to make sure he really left, the urge to run from the risk he posed to her composure was too strong. So she obeyed it, though at as sedate a walk as she could manage.

She clearly needed to spend some time alone reminding herself that unless she was careful, there would always be someone—she realized belatedly she hadn't asked Mr. Tuxedo his name—out there ready, willing and able to use her in some way.

She also needed to remind herself the perfect man didn't exist.

BRENDAN MACDOUGAL STARED after the vulnerable mother cum unyielding neurologist. Curiously, she still clutched his handkerchief in her hand.

He was more than a little surprised and intrigued by the beautiful doctor's abrupt transformation. The soft, beguiling woman who'd made him want to take her in his arms and protect her from the world had turned into an icy bureaucrat with no compunction about tossing him out on his ear.

Her ID badge said her name was Dr. Rose Doeber. All sorts of metaphors involving petals and thorns came to mind. The woman took his brain in the damnedest directions.

Just the sight of her remarkable blond hair shining in the soft, bedside light as she sat, head bowed, next to the sleeping child had been enough to bring a screeching halt to his trek down the long, deserted hall earlier.

He'd spent more than a little time in the presence of women who used a lot of their energy pampering themselves with expensive treatments to get their hair to look like the proverbial spun gold, or silk, or the liquid sunshine he'd had the nerve to compare some women's hair to when he was younger. But he'd never seen hair like hers. The light had shimmered on the smooth golden strands, beckoning his touch.

Then he'd noticed her shoulders shuddering beneath her blue shirt, and heard her crying.

The muscles in his stomach clenched at nothing

more than the memory. The soft, muffled sound had drawn him to her with the same compulsion as a panicked cry for help would have.

He'd immediately thought the little boy with the same silky blond hair as hers had been gravely injured or ill, but his chubby arms, wrapped around a worn-looking stuffed rabbit, were free of IV tubes. No rhythmic beeps from monitoring equipment competed with the heart-rending noises Dr. Doeber had been making.

Thanks to his two younger sisters, Brendan knew a woman didn't cry like that without a reason.

So he'd intruded.

But his attempt to cheer her up had failed. His usually reliable charm had taken a hike when he saw how beautiful she was, despite the red splotches on her cheeks and at the end of her finely shaped nose. And her lack of husband or boyfriend had nearly shot his magnanimous motivations to hell.

Brendan pushed his hands into his pant pockets and rocked back on his heels. He and the tempting doctor, who couldn't quite keep the sexy sway out of her authoritative march down the hall, might have more in common than a soft spot for little kids. Her poise and attitude screamed debutante.

Surely she was enough like him that he could trust her. The hint of vulnerability he'd glimpsed in her soft blue eyes before she shut him out seemed to be doing a good job keeping at bay the cynicism that hit him lately whenever he met a gorgeous woman. He'd found out firsthand how a pretty face could hide a scheming heart.

Unfortunately, he didn't think he'd have an easy time getting her to trust him. At least, not enough to gain her cooperation.

The cell phone in his breast pocket vibrated. He took it out and checked the number. Rory.

Brendan pushed the button and answered with a quiet, "Hey."

"Where'd you go?"

"The hospital. I figured I'd get a jump on things for tomorrow."

His brother was silent for a moment. "I couldn't hear what was going on at your end of the table. Did it get that bad?"

The tension that had been riding Brendan with an iron hand since he'd escaped the formal dinner party–turned–inquisition returned and brought his shoulders up. "And then some."

He'd expected wariness from the donors at the dinner who had once been generous to his family's charitable foundation. But he hadn't been prepared to have his own integrity and maturity so openly doubted.

Rory's noisy sigh sent static over the connection. "You just need to hang in there, Bren. You'll change their minds. You know you will. Then you can get your butt back to New York."

The tightness migrated to Brendan's jaw. "But there's no changing the fact that I *am* only thirty years old and was the one who'd approved giving millions to Rebecca Crestfield." Ms. Crestfield was the self-proclaimed "Patron of the Windy City's Poor," a woman who'd turned out to be the worst sort of scam artist.

Rebecca had cast her line and he'd swallowed the hook on the first pass. He'd fallen for her. Hard. So much so that he'd started planning their future together. Something he'd never done before.

Too bad she was already married.

Then she and her husband took off with every cent they'd raised for the hospital wing expansion, leaving Brendan's reputation in tatters and a bitter burn deep in his chest.

He would never, ever trust, let alone love, a woman that way again, unless he knew everything there was to know about her.

Brendan gave a quieter version of his brother's sigh. "I can't go home until I repair the damage done to the MacDougal Foundation's credibility here in Chicago. I need to regain at least a portion of our major donors' trust."

He'd worked long and hard doubling the size of the pediatric programs in several big-city hospitals, proving to his folks they'd been right to trust him to run the MacDougal Foundation. And he'd been so close to pulling it off here, too.

Rory said, "You will. Don't worry. Tomorrow's photo shoot will help."

"I know. And I appreciate you helping me out."

"No sweat."

Hopefully the positive publicity Rory's cachet as a famous NASCAR driver generated would reassure the donors Brendan had spent the past year cultivating. And when they saw Dr. Doeber's adorable little patient, they'd surely put a lock on it. "I found the perfect kid to be in the pictures with you. His name is Dylan, he's cute as hell and his health won't be compromised by his involvement."

"Sounds great."

"I just have to get his doctor to change her mind about letting me seek the parents' permission." Brendan shifted his attention down the hall, where the leggy blond doctor had disappeared, unsure how best to approach the problem.

His brother made a disparaging noise.

Brendan chided, "Hey, you know my motto. With enough charm and money, anything is possible."

"Whatever. In case I've gone to bed before you get back, I'm going to pack up my stuff so I can leave right from the shoot, okay?"

"That's fine."

"Later."

"Later, Rory." Brendan turned off his phone. He

heard a deep chuckle. The nurse he'd winked at earlier stood in the door of the room opposite Dylan's.

"Sweetheart," she said, "there'll be no changing that one's mind. They don't call her Dr. Doberman for nothing."

Dr. Doberman.

Another intriguing direction. And a challenge if he'd ever heard one.

Brendan relaxed his stance and gave the older woman a wicked grin. Affecting the Scottish accent used by younger members of his family as a joke, he retorted, "Ah, but she's never met a MacDougal before, now, has she?"

Chapter Two

Rose made the drive from her Chicago-style bungalow in Evanston to the hospital on autopilot, despite the newness of the journey. It had only been a month since she'd moved from her studio apartment near the hospital to the nicest close-in suburb she could afford. Hopefully the change would prove just how ready she was to make Dylan a part of her life.

Thank goodness the old but reliable BMW she'd bought off a cash-strapped anesthesiologist knew the way, because she couldn't keep her thoughts from the man who had walked out of the shadows last night, as if he'd stepped straight from some deeply held fantasy she'd never imagined having.

She glanced at the passenger seat, where the handkerchief she'd stormed off with the night before lay on top of her oversize backpack, the quality of the pure white, fine cloth blatant against the faded black nylon of the bag. The elegant block style of the monogram was distinctly male and undeniably extravagant.

BLM.

Each time her mind started to wander to the possible names those initials stood for, she shut herself down by substituting *Bureau of Land Management.* Nothing mysterious or romantic about that.

It was bad enough she'd carefully hand washed the silly thing in her bathroom sink at two in the morning. At first she'd been reluctant to remove the faint spicy scent still clinging to the handkerchief, but she was determined to return it to him clean, carrying no reminders of what had transpired between them.

Because he'd wanted to use Dylan in a photo shoot. He was undoubtedly a man accustomed to using people.

That had ended her fantasy abruptly. She didn't want him to think he was connected to her in any way because she'd allowed him to comfort her for a few minutes.

But in the future she sure as heck would make certain to break down only behind locked doors, where handsome strangers couldn't come across her and try to coax her into giving them what they wanted. Her foster parents, an attractive couple who had wooed her into choosing them from the many qualified applicants, had wanted the fame attached to coming to the rescue of "Little Lost Rose." If

Dylan was used in a publicity campaign, he might suffer the same sort of fate, only wanted for his notoriety.

She wouldn't allow it.

After reaching the hospital, she stuffed the linen square in the pocket of her lab coat. She'd drop the handkerchief off at the pediatric nurses' desk, with instructions to return it to him or to one of his "people" when he showed up for the photo shoot.

A man who looked as suave and confident as he had and wore a tuxedo like his, perfectly tailored to his broad shoulders and narrow waist, most definitely had "people."

Her jaw set, she strode into the hospital through the back entrance, and made her way to the ped wing.

Rose halted not two steps out of the stairwell closest to the pediatric ward nurses' station and closed her eyes. A sea of flowers? The door to the stairs fluttered her hair as it swung closed, barely missing her. Having to question her sanity twice within seven hours was a bit much.

Though she shouldn't be surprised after the night she'd had, her dreams filled with grown-up wants and needs, not childhood terrors and anxieties. A first for her.

But when she opened her eyes, it still looked as if she'd mistakenly stepped into the hospital's florist.

Except the shop in the lobby never had this many roses on hand. Never.

They were everywhere. Two, three deep on the counter rimming the circular nurses' station, covering the floor in front of the counter and filling several carts parked along the wall. Rose took a few tentative steps forward, her senses overwhelmed by the profusion of color and fragrance. Each bouquet was made up entirely of one color and type of rose, everything from deep red blooms with long stems to exquisitely delicate white miniatures.

Her skin prickled with foreboding, but she ignored the sensation. Finding a space between two tall vases crammed with long-stemmed roses—one all vibrant pink, the other graduating shades of orange—she peered through and found Delores doing paperwork. Her shift was almost over.

"Which celebrity's kid is sick, and why in the heck is he or she here?" Rose asked. Chicago General's pediatric floor was woefully behind the times, and not popular with parents who could afford to send their kids elsewhere.

Delores looked up over her reading glasses and scanned the wall of flowers. Her gray brows came together as she let out an exasperated breath. "Where are you, Dr. Doeber?"

Rose stuck her hand between two vases and wiggled her fingers. "Here."

Delores pushed herself to her feet and tried looking over the flowers. Rose stood on tiptoe as well.

"Ah. There you are. The only celebrity we have around here is you, apparently. These are all for one Dr. *Rose* Doeber."

Rose dropped to her heels almost as hard as the dread hit the pit of her stomach. She'd done her best to bury her past and the notoriety she'd suffered as a child. Who other than Delores and Dr. Williams, the head of pediatrics, knew her secret?

Delores chuckled from the other side of the roses. "It seems you weren't sufficiently impressed by the tuxedo last night."

The prickly foreboding she'd felt earlier turned into a flaming rash. "These are from—"

"Me," said a deep, smooth voice she'd know anywhere. A voice she would forever link with the night.

She whirled and found Mr. Bureau of Land Management not two feet from her, his hands behind his back. He no longer sported a tuxedo, but there was no mistaking him. His light brown suede jacket drew the eye to his broad shoulders, and screamed classy casual like only designer clothes could. His chocolate-brown crew-neck shirt and matching slacks set off his hazel eyes and thick, dark brown hair. His fingers had made tracks through his hair where he'd styled it back from his face.

She tucked her own tingling fingers into the pockets of her lab coat. In the left pocket she felt the soft linen of his handkerchief, a poor substitute for his hair.

He nodded at the flowers on the counter. "I instructed them to send the bouquets to your office."

"Like they'd fit. Besides, I don't have a regular office. I haven't finished my fellowship yet."

Delores spoke from somewhere among the flora. "Mr. MacDougal seems to think he can change your mind about something." She chuckled again. "Poor boy."

MacDougal. Rose would have never come up with that name as part of the monogram. Unfortunately, it was a heck of a lot more romantic than *Management.*

He extended his hand. "Brendan MacDougal. It's a pleasure to meet you, Dr. Doeber."

Brendan. That just left the *L.* She pushed away the stupid thought and ignored his outstretched hand. "Is that true, Mr. MacDougal? Did you think I could be swayed to change my mind about what is best for one of my patients by..." She pulled her hands from her pockets and spread them wide, but was still unable to encompass them all. "Where in the world did you get so many roses so quickly?"

He grinned, causing her to doubt her sanity for the third time. No man was that good-looking in real life.

"I told you, I'm very resourceful. The flower

market opens extremely early for florists, and I happen to know a good florist.'' He stepped closer.

Rose stepped back, right into a bouquet of yellow roses. Her composure slipped further as she scrambled to halt a rose domino effect. It would have been funny if Dylan weren't involved.

The vases steadied again, she turned and straightened with as much dignity as she could muster. ''I'm sorry, but it'll take a lot more than…'' she looked around in disbelief ''…hundreds of roses to change my mind.''

He had the grace to appear contrite. ''I was afraid of that. So I picked this—'' he produced a single yellow daffodil from behind his back ''—myself.''

Stunned and touched by the sweet simplicity of the gesture, Rose found herself accepting the flower he offered. She met his gaze and allowed herself a moment lost in the tangle of golds, browns and greens blended together in the warmest hazel eyes she'd ever seen.

Had he been after just about anything else, she might have reconsidered. ''Dylan is still off-limits to you, Mr. MacDougal.''

He didn't look convinced. In fact, his grin canted off to the side and his lids lowered partway in a suggestive expression. ''But what about you, Dr. Doeber?''

Rose swallowed and stepped to the side, away from both the flowers behind her and the temptation in front of her. Boys and men had been fleeting in her life, only welcome until questions about her past became too difficult to brush off, until they got close enough that it would hurt when it ended. Relationships were the only thing in this world she'd admit she ran from.

She glanced at the clock above the nurses' station. "I'm sorry, Mr. MacDougal, but I really don't have time for this." Dylan would surely be awake by now. Knowing he would love the daffodil, she said, "I'll accept this flower, but I can't accept the rest."

"That's fine. I'll have them distributed among the patients."

Another unexpected and touching gesture. She shoved it aside, too. "They will be appreciated. Goodbye, Mr. MacDougal." This time she stood her ground to make sure he left.

He inclined his head. "Dr. Doeber." Then he turned and walked away, not looking defeated in the least. He probably didn't know how.

Having cleared a space among the bouquets so she could watch the show, Delores nailed Rose with an exasperated look over the top of her reading glasses. "When are you going to learn that there's more to life than what goes on here?"

Considering Rose's life *was* here as long as she was forced to prolong Dylan's hospital stay to keep him out of foster care, she disregarded the comment and held up the daffodil. "Do you have a vase handy?"

Delores rolled her dark eyes and grumbled something about youth being wasted on the young as she retrieved an empty bud vase. But the way she looked at Rose when she handed her the vase made it clear she knew exactly why Rose was back at the hospital long before her next scheduled shift. "He had a good night."

Rose let out a relieved breath and nodded in acknowledgment. Delores was the main reason Rose was able to leave the hospital at all. Nightmares weren't allowed on her watch.

"Dr. Williams—" Delores began, but the shrill buzz of a call button cut her off. She smiled indulgently when she saw which room it had come from. "Miss Taylor means it when she says she has to go to the bathroom the second she wakes up. I'll be right back." She waded through the flowers and headed down the hall.

Rather than wait for Delores to return, Rose went in the opposite direction, toward Dylan's room. He rarely slept past seven-thirty and she didn't like him to wake up alone.

Despite her eagerness to see her little boy she quietly entered the room he usually had to himself, thanks to Dr. Williams's indulgence.

The bed was empty.

Her smile faltered, then she shook her head. He

must be in the bathroom—playing in the sink or unwinding the toilet paper. He hadn't shown any interest in potty training, but he just loved to make a mess. In that respect he was a completely normal three-year-old.

She set her backpack on a chair and peeked around the door. The bathroom was empty, too. Her heart rate picked up and a cold fist of anxiety grabbed hold of her stomach.

She left the daffodil and vase on the vanity and searched the room again, even checking the closet— just like the one where the police had first discovered Dylan. The thought of him being that frightened again because he'd woken up alone crowded the air from Rose's lungs.

She whirled and made another, more frantic search of the room, finally noticing that the side rail on Dylan's bed had been lowered, something he couldn't have done on his own. And his bunny was still on the bed. He never went anywhere by himself without Bunny.

Someone had taken Dylan from his room.

A rawer, base panic flooded her system faster than a main-lined drug. What if his caseworker had seen through Rose's efforts to keep Dylan out of the foster care system until she could adopt him? She couldn't let Dylan think she'd abandoned him. She'd rather die than have him go through that kind of upheaval and uncertainty.

She tore out of the room and ran for the nurses' station, arriving the same time as Delores. Rose's running shoes squeaked on the linoleum when she stopped at the ring of flowers. "Where's Dylan?"

The head nurse raised a calming hand. "That's what I started to tell you when Miss Can't Wait buzzed me. Dr. Williams came by about—" she looked up at the large wall clock behind Rose "—oh, twenty minutes ago." She leaned close and grinned. "He'd heard about the flowers."

Rose closed her eyes and silently groaned. She was sure to get another lecture about her choices in life.

"Dylan was awake and a little out of sorts, so Dr. Williams took him for a walk to cheer him up. Said he had a surprise for our little angel."

In a flash Rose's panic turned to a guttural fear. Dr. Williams had once led her from her hospital room to his office with a surprise for her.

A family to call her own.

A family that hadn't lasted.

The couple who had taken her in as their foster child, claiming to be so eager to adopt her, had eventually abandoned her, too. They'd decided that a stubborn, moody preteen was too much to handle after the notoriety attached to the long process of adopting Rose Doe had worn off. The process had been halted, and with a last name of her own making, she'd been sent back to the state, to the roulette wheel of foster care.

Rose wouldn't let the same thing happen to Dylan.

She spun on her heel to race to Dr. Williams's office and instead knocked over a vase, spilling water and peach-colored roses along with her irrationality.

Dr. Williams hadn't come to get Dylan.

He was well aware of how much she loved that little boy, how much kinship she felt with him. Hadn't he proved as much by allowing her to keep Dylan a patient at the hospital while she ran what were technically outpatient tests on him?

Dr. Williams had come to see the spectacle Brendan MacDougal was making of her in an attempt to get her to change her mind about the photo shoot.

This time Rose did take off, jumping over the spilled water and flowers and running for the stairs. She was winded, despite the fact she normally took the stairs to avoid the "what did you do this weekend" elevator chitchat she never had an answer to other than "I worked." She paused on the ground floor landing.

The rational part of Rose's brain rushed to reassure her that the "surprise" Dr. Williams had mentioned was simply a chance for Dylan to see what was going on. Not participate.

The part of her that had learned the hard way

never to trust said *Yeah, right*. It didn't take a stretch of the imagination to believe that Brendan Mac-Dougal would still find a way to get exactly what he wanted.

Rose abandoned any semblance of control as she ran for the main entrance of the hospital, dodging carts and slow-moving patients without excusing herself.

She couldn't let reporters take Dylan's picture with some famous race car driver. Dylan's father, Bobby Ray, might see the photos and decide the child he'd never laid eyes on, the child he'd cared as much for as the young woman he'd hooked on drugs, then left to die, was worth something to him after all. He could change his mind about signing the papers he'd sworn he'd finally get around to signing, even if the only thing in it for him was his fifteen minutes of fame. And Dylan would be left in the same limbo Rose had spent her life in.

He might not be as lucky as she'd been in the end, guided to pursue a career she could pour her heart and soul into. She was able to understand the fears and uncertainties of her little patients from firsthand experience. She knew what it was like to be unable to remember.

She came at the wide, automatic glass doors of the hospital's main entrance at an angle to avoid the security guard directing people to a different way out. She ducked behind him, and the doors had barely opened before she slipped through.

The sight that greeted her brought her up short.

A NASCAR race car painted bright blue, green and yellow, and covered with sponsors' decals for everything from motor oil to prescription allergy medicine was parked in the grassy center of the circular drive and gleamed in the spring morning sun. A crowd of people standing in bunches had gathered on the side of the car farthest from her. A bald photographer in head-to-toe khaki stood between the crowd and the car. He lowered his camera and straightened from his hunkered-shoulder stance to wave her out of his shot.

Rose's gaze dropped to where he had been aiming his lens and her heart stalled. Dylan was inside the race car, sitting on the lap of a dark-haired man in a racing jumpsuit who closely resembled Brendan MacDougal.

The boy's smiling face had been lit from below by some sort of light in the car's cab, so there was no doubting it was him. Both of his little hands were on the steering wheel as if he was driving, and he was bouncing up and down in obvious delight.

Her wishes—no, make that her *orders*—that Dylan not be used in the shoot had been ignored. Or countermanded, she thought as she remembered who had brought Dylan out here in the first place.

She yanked her gaze from Dylan to search the

crowd behind the photographer. She immediately spotted Dr. Williams, a tall, robust man with a full head of silver hair that made him hard to miss. Didn't he realize how using Dylan in this sort of publicity stunt might endanger her chances of adopting him?

Her gaze shifted to the handsome, even taller man standing next to her mentor. Her vision narrowed as her blood pressure skyrocketed.

Not from attraction. Her blood boiled because he'd gone over her head to get what he wanted. Maybe Dr. Williams hadn't countermanded her, after all. Maybe Mr. *MacDougal* hadn't bothered to mention that he'd spoken to her twice already.

That she'd told him no.

A security guard was moving toward her, urging her to clear the area between the race car and the hospital's main entrance, while the photographer continued to wave her off. Rose ignored them both and instead marched straight toward the car, intending to remove Dylan from the threat the media exposure held.

People started shouting at her then, but she had no trouble turning a deaf ear to their voices as she rounded the sleek, gaudy car and approached the open driver's-side window. Dylan spotted her and grinned wider, slapping the steering wheel so she'd be sure to see what he was doing.

Rose smiled despite her anger as she reached for

him. She had to get him away from all these people. Away from the *spectacle.*

Dylan reared back against the chest of the race car driver—Rory, if she remembered correctly. Rose realized she'd seen him on television, either racing or doing promotions. He bore enough handsome similarities to her man in a tux to make it obvious they were brothers, even though the lines bracketing his full mouth made him seem older and less inclined to smile than his brother.

He certainly wasn't smiling now. "Is there a problem?" His voice was deep and rough, as if he'd spent too much time yelling over the roar of the car's engine. Very unlike his brother's silky smooth baritone, which was undoubtedly perfectly suited to getting his way in the dark.

Fighting the image of Brendan MacDougal whispering to her from the pillow next to hers, she snapped, "I'm afraid so." She reached for Dylan again. "Come here, honey."

The little boy shook his head adamantly, gripping the steering wheel for all he was worth, and Rose couldn't bring herself to yank him out of the car. Dylan's being there wasn't the issue; it was the pictures they were taking of him.

She whirled on the photographer. "No more pictures. I mean it."

He frowned and spread his arms, then turned toward the man she felt sure was responsible for the situation, who was approaching with Dr. Williams.

Assuming Mr. MacDougal had neglected to mention that she'd already refused when he'd asked for permission to use Dylan in the shoot, she addressed Dr. Williams. "Last night, I told him—" she nodded toward the taller man, no less compelling by daylight in casual clothes than at night in a tux "—that he couldn't use Dylan in his circus."

Dr. Williams gave her the paternal, patient look that used to be her anchor in the storms of her life, many of her own making. Today it set her teeth on edge. "I know you did."

She blinked. "What?"

"Mr. MacDougal told me that you had placed Dylan 'off-limits.'"

"Then why is Dylan in the car having his picture taken?"

Dr. Williams heaved a sigh. "Rose, this campaign, run by Mr. MacDougal here, is making our new pediatric wing possible through the venerable MacDougal Foundation."

Rose swallowed. She'd heard of the MacDougal Foundation. More than a few pediatric programs across the country had benefited from its generous grants and fund-raising campaigns. Why hadn't she put two and two together?

Shifting to his patented "no arguments" look, Dr. Williams said, "And Dylan is out here because when I stopped by his room looking for you, I found him crying in his bed.''

While he'd said it matter-of-factly, without censure, Rose still mentally flailed herself for being late this morning.

As if he knew what she was thinking, Dr. Williams sighed in exasperation and continued. ''I figured coming out here to see the race car would cheer him up. Which it did. So much so that the second I put him down he ran straight for the car and wanted in.'' The memory softened the lines on Dr. Williams's face. ''Rory obliged, and the photographer started taking pictures.''

Dr. Williams pointed a thumb at the man next to him. ''Brendan initially called a halt to it, saying you'd forbidden Dylan's participation, but I told them to go ahead.''

''You—but—'' she stammered. ''What if—''

Dr. Williams held up a hand. ''I see no harm in it, Doctor, and I'll make the necessary phone calls before the photos are used.'' To Mr. MacDougal he said, ''Dylan is a ward of the state.''

MacDougal's eyebrows went up—along with Rose's blood pressure.

To her, Dr. Williams said, ''Besides, it will be good for the hospital.''

Rose clenched her teeth and struggled to keep her frustration from showing. Especially to this MacDougal, who was watching her a little too intently.

He looked as if he was waiting for steam to come out her ears.

She threw him her most brittle smile instead. "I see." She looked back at Dr. Williams and willed him to understand but kept her tone and expression as professional as possible. "May I remind you, Doctor, that what is best for the hospital might not be best for this particular patient."

MacDougal made a subtle but derisive noise and gestured toward Dylan pretending to drive the race car while its usual driver obliged him by making loud car noises. "I've always been under the impression that having the time of your life was a good thing. Especially for your health." He looked back at her and flashed a smile that should have blinded her with its charm.

Instead of blinding her, it raised warning flags to go with the goose bumps on her arms. This one was dangerous. Rose put on a show of lifting her chin and one eyebrow, so he'd be sure to notice how unimpressed she remained.

She couldn't allow herself to be impressed, not with Dylan involved.

Her gaze went involuntarily to his handsome, equilibrium-shattering face and broad shoulders.

But she set her jaw and hardened her resolve. His sexy, come-hither charm wouldn't sway her. There was no way she was going to give in to him now.

He didn't know it yet, but Mr. MacDougal had met his match.

Chapter Three

Brendan had never been so attracted to someone so prickly in his life. Not a good sign. He should walk away from her. Unless he kept it physical. Physical he could do.

He wasn't exactly thrilled about upsetting her—he'd been raised better than that—but damn, mad looked good on her.

She'd been a tear-streaked beauty the night before, her anguish twisting his gut until he wanted to gather her in his arms and protect her from the world. Today she'd been like an avenging angel with her white doctor's coat flapping behind her as she'd charged across the dewy grass toward Rory's race car.

Once Brendan had come close to her, though, she'd reined in her fury enough that most people probably wouldn't realize how ticked she was.

There were only a few hints of the passion fueling the good doctor's anger contained behind a professional facade. The slight pink flush to her sculpted cheeks and slender neck. The flash of heat brightening her incredibly blue eyes. The tremor of emotion that sneaked into her voice as she argued her point about the boy's involvement in the shoot with her boss.

A point that seemed to go beyond the simple fact that she was mad about having her orders overruled.

And Brendan's attempt to charm her only made her bristle more, though he doubted the casual observer—something he apparently was not when it came to this woman—would notice how stiffly she held herself. He knew exactly where to rub if she'd let him, to ease the knots that formed from that kind of tension, exactly where to massage her satiny skin with firm even strokes.

He discreetly pulled at his collar to free some of the excess heat generated by the thought of touching her, because he seriously doubted she would let him. Yet.

With her chin tilted and her brow prettily arched, she asked with only faintly false sweetness, "I'm sorry, but that was *Mr.* MacDougal, wasn't it? Not *Dr.* MacDougal? No? Well then, would you excuse us for a moment while we discuss *my* patient's health and welfare?"

Brendan fought the urge to smile in admiration of her spirit.

Dr. Terence Williams, whom Brendan had been

working closely with since arriving in Chicago last week to do damage control for the foundation, after word of Rebecca's betrayal—and the amount of the hospital fund she'd made off with—got out, gave Dr. Doeber a surprisingly stern look. "Perhaps it would be best if we *didn't* discuss little Dylan's health right now."

The pretty doctor's cool expression thawed a bit and she dropped her chin. She looked almost guilty. Perhaps this wasn't an isolated incident. Perhaps she'd been chastised before.

Dr. Doeber stood silent for a moment, clearly going over her options, then pulled in a noisy breath and raised her head. The fiery determination blazing in her gorgeous eyes was even more intense than before. "You have to agree that this sort of attention isn't good for Dylan right now. After all he's been through, his emotional state is far too fragile to handle this—this—" She waved an impatient hand at the race car, the lights, the crowd.

To lighten the mood, Brendan interjected, "Every boy's dream come true?" He was rewarded with a scathing glare that made him clamp his lips shut. Whoa. What if he could turn all that fire into desire?

He started to get hot under the collar again, and his attention snagged on her lips. The upper one was perfectly bowed, and complemented by a plump lower one. Would they be hard and firm, or soft and yielding? Would she give as well as take? Her lips pursed in obvious displeasure and he jerked his gaze away to rein in his runaway imagination.

Dr. Williams glanced at the little boy, still bouncing on Rory's lap and looking as if he'd never had so much fun. "It'll be fine, Dr. Doeber," he said, giving her a meaningful nod.

"But what if—" She stopped abruptly and took a deep breath, obviously thinking better of continuing to argue with the head of pediatrics. But her frustration was palpable.

Brendan had been around a lot of hospitals and doctors during the past several years, but he'd never encountered a physician so passionate about a relatively trivial matter concerning a patient in her charge. Most likely Dr. Rose Doeber was becoming too attached to the boy.

His gaze traveled over her blond hair, shining in the sunlight much as it had in the glow of the bedside lamp the night before, then her classical features and tall, slender body. She exuded elegance and grace. She was passionate *and* beautiful.

A lightbulb went on in Brendan's head. She'd be a great spokesperson for the foundation. Who better to counter the negative opinions floating around about his judgment and get the fund-raising for the new children's wing back on track than a dedicated pediatric neurologist—a neurologist with the beauty and presence of the most privileged socialite?

She obviously wasn't too pleased with what was

going on at the moment. But if Brendan could convince Dr. Rose Doeber to partner with him during
his fund-raising efforts in the next few weeks, the
stain on his reputation for trusting the wrong sort of
woman might actually have a chance to fade. She
could help him raise a ton of money. And they'd
have to work together closely, of course.

Speculation and anticipation warmed his blood
even more.

Returning his full attention to her, he noticed the
tick in her jaw muscle as she watched her patient
being photographed again in the car with Rory.
Brendan realized getting her to help him with anything wasn't going to be the walk in the park he was
used to with most women.

His mouth twitched with the beginnings of a grin.
The MacDougal charm had yet to completely fail
him. And he'd never been above playing dirty to get
what the foundation, and ultimately a hospital,
needed.

STRUGGLING TO GAIN control of her frustration,
Rose had counted to thirty-eight when Brendan
MacDougal's voice interrupted her.

"You know, Terence…"

She swung her gaze to the source of her problem.
Terence. No wonder the two men were on the same
side. Despite Dr. Williams being the closest thing to
a father figure she'd had in her life, Rose had never

been able to bring herself to call him by his first name. Perhaps the formality made his unwillingness to get married so he could have adopted her all those years ago easier to bear.

But this MacDougal guy was all sorts of buddy-buddy with him. An ancient, bitter jealousy squirmed in her chest. She didn't have that kind of relationship with anyone.

She didn't want that kind of relationship, she reminded herself sternly. Except with Dylan.

Once he had Dr. Williams's attention, MacDougal continued, "Perhaps our fund-raising efforts would be more successful if we had a representative from the hospital's rank and file working with us. Someone with firsthand experience, who could tell potential donors how much the children would benefit if the pediatric wing was expanded. Someone who cares passionately about the children." His gaze drifted to her, followed by Dr. Williams's.

The older man raised a thick silver brow, a speculative glint in his brown eyes, before he faced Mr. MacDougal again. "I think you're right. Do you have anyone in mind?"

MacDougal's gaze slid over her like a caress, then he grinned, his perfect white teeth gleaming in the morning sun as if he were in some sort of tooth whitener commercial. Her stomach flip-flopped, and she told herself it was from disgust. Or dread. She had a sinking feeling she knew what was coming next.

"Actually," he practically purred, with the darnedest, toe-curling sexuality, "I think Dr. Doeber here would be an excellent spokesperson for the staff at Chicago General. Aside from her obvious attributes—"

Surprised by his blatant sexism, Rose quickly raised her eyebrows, ignoring the tingling sensation attacking her skin.

He lowered his own brows in chastisement, but his eyes held a devilish glint. "By which I mean her *professional accomplishments.* She is articulate, determined and clearly committed to her patients. Or at least to that little guy." He finally looked away to gesture at Dylan, who was now sitting on the roof of the race car while its long-limbed, muscular driver climbed out.

Instead of instantly defending herself, she had to use the momentary reprise to emotionally—and physically—regroup. This new tactic of his was the last thing she would have expected.

Dr. Williams firmly said, "Oh, she is extremely dedicated to all her patients. Without exception. And I agree that Dr. Doeber would be the perfect candidate to help you out, since she herself has experience with such funds."

Rose's heart stuttered. Was he going to expose her background as a charity case? She couldn't think of anything worse. Her past had to stay in the past. It was the only way she could deal with it.

MacDougal grinned. "Excellent. I'll just run a quick background check—"

"That won't be necessary," Dr. Williams interrupted.

Rose couldn't so much as make a sound. Her heart had lodged in her throat at the mention of *background check.*

Thankfully, Dr. Williams added, "I will personally vouch for Dr. Doeber, Brendan. She is of exemplary character."

A muscle in his jaw working, MacDougal glanced from her to Dr. Williams before relenting with a quick nod. "I trust your judgment, Terence."

Rose let out the breath she'd been holding. As far as Dr. Williams was concerned, all was forgiven.

Turning to her with an expression that brooked no argument, her mentor said, "Dr. Doeber, I want you to make yourself available as much as possible to the MacDougals, Brendan specifically, and their fund-raising efforts."

She argued anyway. "I couldn't possibly—I mean, my schedule—"

Dr. Williams laid a hand on her shoulder and squeezed gently. "Do it for me."

She exhaled sharply, feeling trapped. Despite everything in her screaming to keep as far away from Brendan L. MacDougal as possible because of the emotions he'd stirred up in her the night before, the pressure of obligation and respect for Dr. Williams had her nodding in agreement. He'd been there for her in the past when she'd had no one, and had guided her into the career she loved.

Brendan smiled again. "Excellent. I know just where we can start. We're hosting a charity auction for the hospital this Friday night, and she can attend as my guest. That sort of thing is probably old hat for her."

Rose struggled to keep the dismay swamping her off her face. He clearly thought her experience in "such funds" had been gained on the donor rather than the receiving side. Granted, it was the far less damaging interpretation, but she'd surely give herself away within five minutes at the auction.

She didn't have a clue about that world of financial and social connections. She'd filled her life with study, to earn scholarships and establish herself in her career. She had made a point of not having any connections whatsoever. It was safer that way.

Scrambling for an excuse, she blurted out, "I can't go. I'm scheduled to work that night."

"I'll find someone to cover for you," Dr. Williams responded calmly.

She ground her teeth and fought the urge to stamp her foot. The only other excuse she could think of just happened to be the truth. "I still can't go. I have nothing to wear and no time to shop."

Dr. Williams said, "I'll see to it that you have the time." His expression stated unequivocally *get a life.*

MacDougal said, "To keep this from being an inconvenience and to expedite matters, I'll gladly take her to a shop I know that has everything she'll need. It's the least I can do."

Dr. Williams gave a satisfied nod. "Brilliant idea. Now, if you'll excuse me, I have some phone calls to make. I'll speak to you later, Brendan." He raised a hand, then headed back toward the hospital's main entrance, in use again now that the photo shoot was wrapping up.

Rose closed her eyes and suppressed a groan. The very last thing she wanted was to go on a *Pretty Woman*-style shopping trip with a man undoubtedly used to that sort of thing. She could easily imagine him lounging in an overstuffed chair in the dressing area of an exclusive boutique while a sophisticated "lady friend" modeled designer gowns—or more likely, judging from the wicked slant of his sensuous mouth, lingerie—for his approval.

Rose's palms grew damp at the thought of his hot eyes on her as she turned slowly for his benefit in nothing but silk and lace.

She opened her eyes and met his gaze directly. "You don't have to go to the trouble."

He arched a brow. "It'll be my pleasure."

Rose swallowed against the longing his words

evoked. There was no question Brendan L. Mac-Dougal knew how to pleasure a woman. She smiled feebly. "I can take care of myself."

"Why should you have to?" he countered, his voice deep and seductively smooth.

She crossed her arms over her chest to ward off his assault on her senses. "Because I want to."

He shifted his weight to one foot and struck a casual pose, but his scrutiny turned steely. "You gave your word. I'm assuming you're a woman of your word."

She opened her mouth to argue that she'd never agreed to the part about him taking her shopping, but he raised his right hand and stopped her, his gold class ring glinting in the sun, much as it had in the lamplight the previous night.

"And just think what good you'll be doing for the children by helping me raise funds for the pediatric wing expansion. For Dylan." There was an unmistakable challenge in his hazel eyes.

Her spine stiffened at his attempt to manipulate her. "The best way I can do good for Dylan is to keep him away from people like you."

His dark brows shot up. "People like me?"

"Yes. People only interested in getting what they want and not caring how they get it."

He bent toward her, bringing his distressingly handsome face close, overwhelming her with his spicy scent and the warmth of his breath. "What I want, Dr. Doeber, is to help the children of this city by providing them with the best medical care possible, in the finest possible facility, equipped with the latest technology. Unfortunately, that takes a lot of money.''

He lifted his broad shoulders in a slight shrug. ''Granted, my family has the wherewithal to donate a large chunk of what is needed, but the rest must come from other donors. Donors who aren't yet aware of how badly their contributions are needed.

''And that's where you and Dylan come in. You can help me get the message out, touch people here.'' He lifted a hand and grazed the space between her left breast and collarbone with his fingertips. ''So they become willing to give some of their hard-earned money to help sick and injured children. Not an easy thing in times like these.''

Rose struggled to think beyond the way her heart was palpitating beneath his electrified touch, to not be affected by it.

She couldn't.

So she stood there like an idiot until he dropped his hand, his fingertips tracing the slightest, almost imperceptible caress down her body before he broke the contact.

''So will you help me, Dr. Doeber? Will you help me help these kids by letting me make you into the most irresistible spokesperson these donors have ever met?''

Suppressing a shiver at what that process could involve, she focused on what mattered. "On one condition."

He straightened, impressive at his full height, but not nearly as imposing to her as when he leaned close. "Which is?"

"You can't use Dylan in the media campaign."

Inhaling noisily, he ran a hand through his hair and turned his attention to the race car. "But look at him."

She did, in time to see Dylan diving from where he sat on the roof of the race car into Rory MacDougal's arms. The older MacDougal ruffled Dylan's wispy hair, then let him scramble headfirst back into the car through the driver's-side window. She hardly doubted he *was* having the time of his life, and a part of her was thankful he'd had this opportunity.

Brendan said, "He's perfect. There is no way the people of the greater Chicago Metro area could look at him and not want to help the hospital."

She jerked her gaze back to the tall man next to her. "The greater Chicago Metro area?"

He glanced at her. "Yeah. Where else?"

"It's a local campaign? Not national?"

"It's hard enough to get the people who actually use the hospital's services to donate money." He scoffed. His expression darkened. "We don't have the resources this time to try to reach people too far away from the hospital and the community it serves.''

"But could that change? Could a picture of Dylan and your brother be used elsewhere?"

He shrugged again. "I suppose it could."

She turned to face him squarely. "Will you swear to me that Dylan's picture will only be used here in Chicago, and nowhere else?"

"Why does it matter?"

She couldn't think of a logical reason quickly enough. "It just does."

He narrowed his eyes and considered her for a moment, then mirrored her action, turning to face her fully. "Will you do all you can to help me raise money for the hospital?"

For Dylan's sake, she swallowed her trepidation and answered firmly. "Yes."

"Okay, then. It's a deal." He stuck out his hand.

Rose hesitated only a moment before slipping hers into his warm, strong grasp, feeling the contact clear to the soles of her feet. Though she hadn't quite succeeded in keeping Brendan L. MacDougal from getting what he wanted, at least she could be sure that Dylan's newfound fame wouldn't reach as far as Folsom Prison.

But as she shook MacDougal's hand, his grip sure, almost possessive, she couldn't help but wonder at what cost to her.

And if maybe, just maybe, she'd met *her* match.

Chapter Four

With the oxford loafers she'd changed into rubbing against her bare heels, Rose paced back and forth in front of the side entrance to the pediatric wing, resisting the urge to check her watch. She doubted more than two minutes had passed since the last time she'd checked it.

Which would make it 8:24 p.m., six more minutes until Brendan L. MacDougal was supposed to pick her up for their grand little shopping spree. With most dress shops closing at nine, it was guaranteed that while buying a dress with Brendan might not be painless, it would at least be quick.

She'd been on edge all day long thinking about doing something so personal with a man as sensual as Brendan. She chewed on her thumbnail, remembering how he hadn't balked this morning when she'd put their shopping trip off until late in the day. He'd initially suggested they leave to go shopping as soon as the photo shoot with his brother finished.

But without Dr. Williams there to contradict her, she'd claimed she was unable to get away from the hospital until this evening.

MacDougal probably figured that, since today was Wednesday, they could go again tomorrow or even Friday if they didn't find just the right dress. He seemed the determined sort.

Little did he know the "right" dress was going to be the first one that fit. Assuming it was plain and simple. Having had her fill of being a source of curiosity when she was younger, she wanted to draw as little attention to herself as possible. Especially from him.

The way he'd looked at her while she was wearing chinos, a plain white blouse and her lab coat was bad enough. She'd been ogled before, but never in a way she could actually *feel,* the way she did when he looked at her. She wrapped her blue flannel blazer closed and held it tight with crossed arms.

Fortunately, the idea of trying on dresses for his approval had kept her from thinking about what it would be like to spend an entire evening with him in his element. She had no doubt that gala events were exactly what he'd been bred for. She'd never been to a single one, and wanted nothing more than to get through the evening without embarrassing herself too much. Just as she wanted to get through this shopping trip as quickly as possible. She would fulfill her end of their bargain, and he'd have to fulfill his.

He'd better.

Brendan MacDougal was all about image. He wouldn't risk his image with the bigwigs she had access to—namely, the hospital board he was trying to raise money for—by reneging on a deal.

At least, she hoped not.

She didn't want to risk her own businesslike image within the hospital's unique society by letting people see her leave with the man who'd created a citywide rose shortage for her. There was enough buzz about all those flowers he'd sent as it was. If he didn't arrive soon, someone was bound to notice her skulking by the side door. She hated to be the object of people's curiosity, rousing questions about her life....

Particularly now when she had so much to lose. She couldn't bear the thought of not being able to adopt Dylan, of not being allowed to give him the kind of life full of love he deserved. The kind she wished she'd had herself.

Tonight's shopping trip was something she had to do for Dylan's sake, and she intended to do it as quickly and as painlessly as possible. Which meant staying immune to BLM's charm and sheer presence. Unfortunately, she had a sinking feeling the only way she'd manage such a feat would be by never looking at him or letting him talk to her.

His voice had lingered in her head all day, the mere memory of his deep, silky tones making her body warm and sensitized. She'd also forgotten to return his handkerchief, and every time she put her hand in her pocket and touched the soft linen she was reminded of him and his compassion. For her own sanity she needed tonight to fly by, not drag along torturously.

A car pulling into the alley between the parking garage and the hospital caught her attention. She checked her watch, which finally read 8:30 p.m. She squinted in the glare of its headlights and fought the urge to smooth her hair as the black sedan pulled almost soundlessly up to her. It was a Mercedes, exactly the sort of car she'd expect from someone connected to the MacDougal Foundation. The guy had to be worth millions.

Except that the man in a dark suit behind the wheel wasn't Brendan MacDougal.

He climbed out. "Good evening, Dr. Doeber," he said.

She stopped and raised her brows at him.

A pleasant-looking man in his mid to late thirties with dark hair, he opened the big car's passenger door with practiced ease and held out a hand to her. A driver. Brendan MacDougal had a driver. Now, if that didn't prove how different she and Brendan were, she didn't know what would. Rose didn't even have a dog.

The tinted rear windows kept her from seeing inside, but the riot of acid in her gut told her who she'd find lounging in the back seat. She took a deep breath and reminded herself she was *not* going to be affected by him.

This was about the deal. Her climbing into this car with him had nothing to do with the two of them personally. Besides, attraction led to wanting, wanting led to having and having led to abandonment. She refused to get caught in that cycle again.

She moved slowly around the open door and bent down to see into the car's interior.

Though he wasn't exactly lounging, Brendan did look extremely at home in the luxury sedan's roomy back seat. He still had on the same dark brown pants, brown shirt and light brown suede jacket, but in the opulent gray leather interior of the Mercedes he looked more suave.

More dangerous to a woman who didn't want to be interested.

Waving away the driver, who was about to help her into the car, she focused on getting in next to Brendan as quickly as she could before they were seen. At least he hadn't come for her in a stretch limo.

The driver closed the door once she had settled in next to Brendan, and the back seat no longer seemed as large as it had before. Even having canted his shoulders to face her, Brendan took up an awful lot of space. His long legs forced him to sit with his knees splayed, and she could feel the heat coming off him. The man was a veritable sexual furnace.

Or maybe she'd been out in the cold for too long. The spicy smell of him alone was enough to make her feel warmer than she ever had before.

He glanced at his watch. "I'm not late, am I?"

"No, you're not late, Mr. MacDougal."

"Please, call me Brendan. Is it all right if I call you Rose, or do you prefer Dr. Doeber?"

Since what she preferred had already gone by the wayside, she simply shrugged. Though the sound of her name on his tongue beat the feeling she got from her favorite dark, creamy chocolate hands down, and she was left with one less barrier between them for her to hide behind.

"You ready to go *shopping?*" Brendan asked with a waggle of his dark brows and an upward curve to one side of his wonderful mouth.

Heat flushed her cheeks as if he'd asked if she was ready to tear one off with him right there in the back seat. An image she probably wouldn't be able to shake for years.

She had to clear her throat before she could answer. "Yes, I'm ready. Let's get it over with."

"You sound like you're on your way to get a root canal." Amusement tinged his deep, smooth voice.

"Frankly, I'd rather have a root canal than go shopping for a dress I won't wear more than once."

He raised one broad shoulder. "Oh, you never know. You might need to dress up some time down the road."

Thinking of the simple life she was working so hard to build for herself and Dylan, she met his twinkling eyes directly. "Trust me, I know."

"Okay. If you say so." He leaned forward to speak to the driver and his warmth and spicy smell engulfed her. "Jeff, could you take us to Oak Street, please?"

"Absolutely, sir."

As the driver headed the car out the other end of the alley Brendan sat back again, but a little more on her side of the car than before. He looked forward as they worked their way into the evening traffic. "So you don't like to shop. That makes you a rare woman."

In his world, maybe. Rose knew plenty of hard-working women who were simply too tired at the end of the day to spend a minute more on their feet.

She kept her attention on the steady stream of traffic outside. "I don't like to waste time on irrelevant things." And the only relevant things in her life were work and Dylan.

From the corner of her eye she saw Brendan turn and look at her. Her skin prickled beneath his scrutiny. "Instilling trust in others by looking your best is not irrelevant."

"I prefer to instill trust by acting trustworthy."

He grunted and shifted in his seat, this time away from her, drawing her gaze despite her best intentions. He watched the traffic crawling along next to them with a surprisingly solemn expression on his face as they made their way toward one of the city's most upscale shopping areas. "Sometimes whether you're trusted or not has nothing to do with your actions and everything to do with how people decide to view you."

She huffed. "In other words, image."

He turned and looked at her, his rich, hazel eyes intense. "Exactly."

While he'd done nothing more than confirm her earlier suspicions about him nearly verbatim, she was strangely disquieted, almost disappointed, by the reality of his concern over image. She shrugged and looked out the window. She didn't want to know why her instincts were screaming that there was more to this man than shallow conceit.

He was surprisingly quiet during the rest of the ride to Oak Street, seemingly lost in his own thoughts. When they pulled up in front of one of the exclusive boutiques lining the street off Michigan Avenue, the driver hurried out to open the rear passenger door. Brendan pulled in a chest-expanding breath, turned and smiled at her, the charm she'd come to expect from him radiating like some sort of aura.

"Here we are. Let's go find the perfect dress for you."

Before she could insist she was more interested in speed than perfection, he climbed out of the sedan and extended a hand to help her.

Steeling herself against the inevitable rush of sensations, she slid across the seat and placed her hand in his. The contact of his skin on hers came as a jolt. The signals her overexcited nerve endings sent out seemed determined to circumvent the rational part of her brain, instead heading straight for every erogenous zone she possessed.

And struck pay dirt.

His palm was warm and his fingers strong but gentle as he balanced her as she climbed out of the car. The second she straightened, she tried to pull her hand from his.

He wouldn't let her. Instead he guided it under his other arm, and placed it inside his bent elbow, holding it there by keeping a seemingly casual hand over hers. The flexed firmness of his biceps and forearm left no doubt as to what filled out his jacket. Rose felt herself heating up, and wished she'd left her blue flannel blazer in her locker at the hospital.

With a satisfied smile, he escorted her into the most incongruous minimalistically posh women's clothing boutique she'd ever seen. Granted, she'd only ever seen expensive boutiques from the outside, as she walked past.

Everything that wasn't a clothing item for sale was stark white. Even the saleswomen were in white, oozing high style from the sleek buns they wore their dark hair in right down to their frighteningly pointy shoes.

The tallest of the three glided over to them. She was a gorgeous woman with jet-black hair and dark, exotic eyes, wearing a perfectly fitted white knit pantsuit with large gold buttons. She glowed with appreciation as she gave Brendan a quick once-over.

Rose's back stiffened automatically. Good heavens—was she so out of control that she was reacting like some sort of territorial female, raising her nonexistent hackles in warning at the approach of a potential competitor? As if Brendan were hers to compete over.

The dark beauty's smile seemed well-rehearsed. "Mr. MacDougal?"

"Yes." He took his hand from Rose's and extended it to the saleswoman.

Rose watched him, but nothing in his handsome profile showed whether he felt at all attracted to the woman, and the handshake was brief. Maybe he didn't flirt with every female he met.

Only those he wanted something from.

The saleswoman spared Rose a brief smile and nod before returning her attention to Brendan. "I'm Clarice. It is such a pleasure to be of service to you." She leaned toward them and lowered her voice. ''As soon as this last customer leaves—'' she unnecessarily indicated a woman in blue at the counter ''—we'll lock the doors and the shop is yours.''

Rose jerked her gaze to Brendan, but he simply tightened the flex of his biceps beneath her hand and inclined his head to Clarice. ''Excellent. Thank you.''

''Our pleasure.''

The woman in blue, who apparently didn't rate the way Brendan did, approached them. Clarice moved to escort her out, locking the door quietly behind the thankfully oblivious shopper. Rose would have hated to make her feel bad.

The two other saleswomen, both brunettes, came sweeping out of a back room they must have ducked into the moment they finished with the other customer, each carrying a silver tray. On one tray were two tall champagne flutes filled to the brim, while the other bore fat, chocolate-dipped strawberries arranged in meticulous rows.

It was all Rose could do not to laugh. The dresses really must be expensive if they had to liquor you up to get you to buy one.

What had she gotten herself into?

Clarice took a glass and held it out to Rose. ''One for the lady.''

Rose used it as an excuse to extract her hand from Brendan's arm.

"And one for the gentleman."

Brendan flashed Clarice a smile of thanks that would have taken a less practiced woman to her knees. Instead Clarice gave him a wicked wink, which Rose was probably not meant to see.

But she *had* seen it, and she found herself taking a drink of the champagne she'd had no intention of drinking. It was either that or succumb to the urge to vent her exasperation by making a rude noise. She told herself it was the triteness of it all that was getting to her.

Clarice said, "Would you prefer to look around and choose the gowns yourselves, or have a seat and allow us to make several selections for you?"

Because Rose intended to choose only one dress, and it certainly wouldn't be a *gown,* she blurted out, "Look around."

At the same moment Brendan said, "Show us your finest."

The women looked back and forth between Rose and Brendan with only the slightest twitch of their sculpted eyebrows.

Brendan turned and considered Rose for a moment. She met his gaze with a studied coolness that had on more than one occasion protected her from people who wanted to get too close.

With a small smile that did worse things to her insides than one of his full-blown sparklers, he inclined his head and said, "You make your own selections, then they'll make a few.'' He hadn't phrased it as a question, but his raised brows suggested he wanted an answer from her.

Since she planned to be long gone before the saleswomen had the chance to select much of anything, she gave him a sweet, patronizing smile and said, ''That would be fine.''

The saleswomen burst into motion, each taking a different wall of the store and whipping long dresses from racks and displays with astonishing speed.

Without bothering to ask her size.

Wide-eyed, Rose glanced at Brendan, who was watching her with a distinctly amused expression as he sipped his champagne.

Not about to be trumped out of her own game, Rose handed Brendan her glass, hustled to the nearest display and started searching for what she considered a run-of-the-mill dress. Unfortunately, this store didn't seem to carry any. Nearly everything was long and gorgeous. And none of the garments had price tags, which made her certain they cost more than her new mortgage payment. Thank heavens she'd bought a home well within her means and had good credit. She'd need it to buy anything in this shop.

She was just starting to sweat when she came to a dressy, black two-piece pantsuit. A pantsuit would work. She would be representing the hospital at the auction, and wearing something more businesslike seemed appropriate. She might even be able to get away with wearing it to staff meetings later on. It wouldn't hurt her to dress up a little every now and again, as long as the outfit wasn't too showy. She'd never fly under the collective radar in Chanel.

She fumbled with the tag. Praise the shopping gods, it was her size. Good thing, because it appeared to be the only one like it hanging there. Which led her to believe it wasn't exactly an "off the rack" sort of item. She pushed her concern about the cost aside and grabbed the pantsuit.

Holding it up in triumph, she announced, "I'll take this one."

The boutique fell eerily silent. Rose looked up to find everyone staring at her.

Brendan cleared his throat and Clarice jumped to life.

"Wonderful. The dressing parlor is right this way." She gestured toward a door draped in white fabric.

Rose turned and headed instead for the high counter that hid the cash register. "That's okay. I don't need to try it on." She hung the suit over her arm and reached into her blazer pocket for her wallet.

Brendan stepped toward her. "You should at least slip into it, Doctor. As you mentioned, you don't have time to come back and exchange it. Nor would you want to spend Friday evening in something that fit poorly.''

Clarice added, ''We certainly don't want you to. Please, it will just take a moment, and then you'll be sure.''

The two other saleswomen chimed in with a chorus of begging.

Rose sighed and relented. She'd still have this ordeal over with in record time. ''All right.'' One thing she'd mastered during her internship was changing her clothes with lightning speed.

Clarice handed her armload of gowns to one of the other women and took the pantsuit from Rose, then led her through the white drapes.

Clarice hadn't been kidding when she called it a *parlor.* It looked much as Rose had figured it would.

The room was large and elegant. Unlike the rest of the store, the lighting was soft, bringing a warm glow to the white walls and plush sage carpet. The owners of the boutique had obviously figured out that women were more likely to be pleased with how they looked in an environment like this rather than the lab motif of the main sales floor.

A glass coffee table and a large, overstuffed chair that matched the carpet commanded the center of the room. Straight ahead was a slightly raised pedestal in a nook lined on three sides with floor-to-ceiling mirrors. The room actually intended for changing, which was more like a normal-size dressing room, lay through another curtain-draped door-way to the right of the mirrored bay.

Clarice hung up the pantsuit, then held the curtain open for Rose. Already shrugging out of her flannel blazer, Rose hustled into the changing room.

Clarice said, "Let me know if you need any assistance."

Though she felt pretty confident she could dress herself, Rose smiled and nodded at her, then pulled the curtain closed. Stepping out of her oxfords and shucking her white blouse and chinos in no time at all, she unfastened the black pants from the hanger and pulled them on.

They nearly fell right back off.

Apparently sizing didn't hold entirely true where high-end fashions were concerned. Unwilling to admit defeat just yet, Rose went ahead and put on the top. Like the pants, it appeared to be at least two sizes too big. She looked pitiful in it, like some underfed waif.

Which she most certainly was not. The hospital cafeteria food and vending machine snacks she lived on were anything but low in calories. Maybe women were willing to fork out more money on clothes if they could wear smaller sizes than usual.

"How does it look?" Brendan's deep voice coming from just the other side of the curtain startled her.

She hesitated. "Ahh…"

"Let me see."

"No."

He was silent for a moment, then asked in a strangled-sounding voice, "Don't you have it on yet?"

"Yes, but—"

"Then let me see." This time his voice was soft and coaxing. Supportive, not challenging. It would seem childish to keep on refusing.

She turned away from the mirror in the small dressing room and yanked open the curtain.

Brendan's eyes widened and he sputtered a laugh, not even trying to be taetful. So much for supportive.

She pulled at the voluminous top. "It's a little big."

He nodded in agreement. "A little. Aren't you glad you agreed to try it on?"

She heaved a sigh of defeat. "Yes."

He cocked a mahogany brow at her, the challenge back in his hazel eyes. "Are you willing to accept help from the experts now?" He gestured toward the threshold of the "changing parlor" where the saleswomen were gathered, wearing the faintest I-told-you-so expressions.

Rose looked wistfully at her watch, then rolled her eyes. "Yes. But I want something…understated. No flash or slink."

Somehow conveying they were offended without actually looking offended, the women brought in the dresses they'd selected, hanging them from the hooks that ringed the large room. Most of the gowns were black, but many were in vibrant jewel tones, and there were even a few pastels. All were gorgeous.

And Rose couldn't tell by looking at them which one would allow her to get through the auction without drawing too much attention to herself. She *would* have to try them all on.

So much for grabbing the first thing she saw and running. She'd failed to keep Brendan MacDougal from getting his way.

Again.

Chapter Five

As one of the saleswomen brought the first gown to Rose, Brendan sat down in the dressing parlor's overstuffed chair and wiped the sweat from his forehead—sweat that had erupted at the thought of Dr. Rose Doeber undressed with nothing more than a curtain between them. His reaction was more intense than when he'd been an inexperienced teenager.

Which he sure as hell wasn't anymore.

But the thought of a tightly wound, controlled woman like Rose peeling off the layers, and maybe her inhibitions, behind a flimsy curtain made him hot.

He took another sip of champagne. Her comments about the relevance of image should have been enough to cool his jets. Actually they had, enough for him to remind himself that until he secured her enthusiasm for the fund-raiser, and thus her effectiveness, he couldn't slack off the charm.

When he'd seen her chinos hit the floor of the

dressing stall—the privacy curtain only went as low as her calf—all thoughts of effective fund-raising had popped like so many champagne bubbles. She had the sexiest legs and feet. The red paint on her toenails had been a shocker after her "I don't waste time on irrelevant things" spiel. He'd been drawn to the curtain like a moth to a flame.

And he was feeling decidedly singed.

He needed to stay focused on bringing her fully on board for Friday's auction. He needed this charity's potential donors to trust his judgment again as much as he trusted Williams's. Or he'd be washed up in the only career he'd ever wanted.

ROSE GROUND HER BACK TEETH together as she watched Clarice place a long, sleeveless black dress with wide straps on the hook where she'd first hung the suit. One of the other saleswomen followed with a pair of classically elegant black high heels, not surprisingly in Rose's size.

Rose obliged by heading back into the dressing stall to take off the ill-fitting pantsuit. As she closed the curtain, she saw that Brendan had sat down in the changing parlor's only chair, just feet from where she was about to get undressed again.

She paused with a hand on the curtain. "What are you doing?"

He arched a brow at her and made a sweeping gesture. "Taking a load off."

"In here?"

Stretching his long legs out in front of him, he said, "Looks to me like the best seat in the house."

Rose shook her head. "No no no no. I'm going to be changing, right here." She gestured to the stall. "Behind this." She flicked the edge of the white curtain. It wasn't see-through, but it didn't go all the way to the floor or to the sides. There would be gaps, spaces were he might catch a flash of her white panties...

He blinked at her lazily.

...which wouldn't impress him at all. She groaned at her own ridiculousness and yanked the curtain closed in front of her. It opened on the other side. His grin widened. This might be a new experience for her, but he looked a little too at home for this to be his first time in the changing room of a women's boutique.

Just get it over with.

She closed the other side more gently and turned her back to the curtain, undressing again as fast as she could. After stripping off the oversize suit and hanging it on the hook rather than taking the time to replace it properly on its hanger, she shimmied into the black dress and pulled the zipper up as far as she could.

It fit. Beautifully.

The princess seaming down the sides made the medium-weight fabric mold perfectly to her breasts and waist without being too tight, and the rest of the gown draped easily over her hips and bottom, roomy enough that it didn't need a slit. The only problem was she felt far too exposed without sleeves, even though the straps were more than wide enough to cover her bra straps, and the neckline was perfectly modest. Wearing a sleeveless sundress or tank top in the middle of summer like everyone else was one thing, but it was only May, and the men would be in suits, maybe even…

Holding the curtain in front of her, she stuck her head out of the changing stall and asked Brendan, "Are you wearing your tuxedo Friday?"

He nodded. "Afraid so. We decided to add weight to the evening by making it formal."

"Oka-a-a-y." She drew the word out, eyeing the other dresses hanging around the room. To Clarice, who was waiting in the doorway to the boutique with the other saleswomen, Rose said, "Do you have anything with long sleeves? I'll freeze in this one."

Brendan sat forward. "You have it on already?"

She nodded, but held the curtain in place. She was *not* putting on a fashion show. The thought of those glowing hazel eyes on her, heating her skin without actually touching her, was enough to turn her into a coward.

He beckoned to her. "Let's see it."

"No."

Clarice, frozen in the act of separating a gown from a bunch hanging near the door, asked, "Doesn't it fit?" Clearly she'd expected it to. Being able to accurately guess a customer's size and shape was probably a major job requirement in a place like this. An incorrect estimate would be tantamount to making a misdiagnosis in Rose's profession.

Rose was quick to reassure her. "No, that's not the problem. I'd just prefer sleeves."

Noisily releasing a pent-up breath, Clarice finished extracting the black dress she'd been after and started toward Rose.

Brendan raised his hand to stop her. "Let her come get it. I want to see everything she tries on."

Rose gaped for a second at his audacity, then glared at him. "What makes you think I want to show you?"

"I know you don't. But I also have the feeling you might be too harsh a judge when it comes to what looks good on you. Let us help you decide." He waved her out again. "Come get this other dress."

One of the saleswomen added, "And the mirrors and lighting here—" she pointed at the bay of mirrors surrounding the raised platform "—are far superior to what's in where you are." She flashed a smile at Brendan, obviously trying to win his approval at the least, or better yet, his notice.

Unexpected anger bubbled in Rose's chest at the

woman's flirting. She slipped on the heels, which also fit, shoved the curtain aside and came out. They might be able to force her to come out of the changing room, but there was no way she was going to pose on a pedestal for them.

Clarice promptly made a liar out of Rose by rushing toward her and hustling her up onto the platform. But not before Rose had a chance to see Brendan's eyes widen and his sensuous mouth curl in what she at first thought was appreciation of what he saw. Then his brows flattened and he brought a finger up to his lips.

Heat flooded her cheeks. When she caught sight of her reflection in the mirrors she was appalled to see how flushed she looked.

"Nice," Clarice murmured, adjusting the fall of the skirt over Rose's hips. "Nice." She smoothed one of the straps. She circled around and got personal by straightening the seams over Rose's breasts. "Nice."

Rose assumed she meant the dress, but blushed more.

Brendan made a clucking noise from his throne behind her. "She deserves much more than 'nice.' This one doesn't do much for me."

Rose just wanted down and out of the spotlight. She didn't let herself consider what Brendan meant, or dare to look at either him or his reflection. The second Clarice moved to the side, Rose stepped off the platform. "I'd still prefer something with sleeves." She reached for the velvet dress over Clarice's arm, but the woman insisted on taking it into the changing room and hanging it up herself. She whisked the suit away like yesterday's garbage.

Rose went straight into the changing stall and put on the next floor length black dress. It had long sleeves, all right. But no back. Absolutely none. It was more fitted than the first thanks to a bit of stretch in the velvet, and the back of the dress was cut in a V, plunging below the waistband of her white bikini underwear. Oh sure, she'd blend in wearing this.

Rose called, "Anything *else* with sleeves of some sort?"

"I'm sure there is, but you'll have to come out in what you have on to get it."

Groaning, Rose jerked the curtain open and went out, keeping a hand over the base of the V where her underwear showed. There wasn't much she could do about the back of her white bra save take the bra off, which she wasn't going to do.

Brendan cocked his head, considering the front of the gown as she emerged from the changing stall. "I like the richness of the fabric, but overall the dress is rather—*hello!*" he exclaimed when she'd walked by far enough for him to see her back. "I don't suppose you'd consider that one, would you, Rose?"

"No." Her cheeks burned, but something close to pleasure at his appreciation expanded in her chest. He wasn't playing Casanova as she'd feared he might, but he didn't appear to be completely unimpressed by her, either. It felt good to wield a little feminine power, especially over a man who was so used to being in control.

She avoided Clarice this time, simply snatching the next gown off the nearest hook. Sleeves clearly didn't equal coverage.

She soon found out that coverage didn't always equal decency. The deep maroon gown she'd grabbed, though sleeveless, had a mock turtleneck, which she at first hoped would make it a winner. But its stretchy fabric clung so tightly that even the little bow on her bra stood out between her breasts. The look was so absurd—or maybe it was the stress of the day getting to her—that she started to giggle.

From the other side of the curtain Brendan asked, "What's so funny?"

Mindful of the delicate egos of the saleswomen, she answered in a stage whisper. "This dress."

"What about it?" His voice sounded closer, conspiratorial.

"I've worn latex gloves that were looser." She giggled again.

"Now, I've got to see that. You decent?"

Her giggle exploded into a laugh.

"Here I come." Brendan stuck his head through

the curtain. In the mirror Rose watched his dark brows hit his hairline at the sight of her encased in the dress.

She stopped laughing, waiting for a well-rehearsed remark about her curves, or how she wasn't supposed to wear undergarments with a dress like this. A much-needed reminder of the roles they were playing here, of the deal they'd made.

One corner of his mouth kicked up. "No offense, but you pretty much look like a beef stick. A sexy beef stick, but a beef stick all the same."

She stared at him a second. The unexpectedness of his remark, not to mention its accuracy, made her burst out laughing harder than before.

He came right into the dressing stall, glass of champagne in hand. He filled the small space completely with his size and presence, much as he'd filled the back seat of the car. And she reacted to him the same way—increased pulse, temperature, her skin tingling with awareness.

She amended her earlier thought that this man had been bred for gala events. He'd been bred for seduction. That, coupled with his humor, made Rose feel woefully unarmed.

He gently took hold of the fabric covering her ribs and pulled on it, releasing it with a snap. "The miracles of modern technology."

Trying to ignore the heat of his body and the

sweet smell of champagne on his breath, she added, ''Not always for the better.''

''Oh, I don't know. I happen to really like beef sticks.'' He flattened his hand against her ribs, then ran it downward to her waist and over her hipbone. His touch was light and nonthreatening. And incredibly erotic.

Her mouth went dry.

Catching her gaze in the mirror, he moved closer and brought his face nearer hers. ''While this dress is tight enough and your figure gorgeous enough to definitely make men willing to part with their money, I'm afraid it would also make their wives not let them. Do you need help getting it off?''

His offer shook her out of the stupor induced by his nearness. She shrugged to encourage him to move back. ''Like I was considering it,'' she croaked. ''And no, I don't need help getting it off.'' She hoped.

He grinned at her and she realized he'd been teasing. She looked down and fidgeted with the dress. She didn't have any experience with being teased. Being dressed up and put on display, yes. Teased, no. And, ridiculously, she found herself wanting more.

''Look,'' he said, regaining her attention. His expression more serious, understanding, and the golds, browns and greens in his eyes drew her in like a hypnotist's charm. ''I know this isn't a whole lot of fun, especially when you have other responsibilities. But the time you spend picking out the right dress will be worth the boost to your comfort level at the auction. I promise.''

She didn't respond, because she had no response to his unexpected understanding.

He sighed. ''You've been at this for a while. Here.'' He handed her the champagne.

She took the flute, then looked from it to the dress. ''I'm not *that* talented.''

He chuckled. ''I suppose you do need both hands to get out of that thing. Have a sip, and I'll take the glass out.''

While she certainly wasn't a drinker, Rose did need something to wash away the desires he'd stirred up. As she tipped the flute to her lips she noticed Brendan watching her mouth, his own lips moving slightly, and her body responded to his hot gaze. She downed practically all the champagne in one gulp.

He was so sexy, so compelling simply standing there, that Rose knew it was going to be difficult to keep him from getting under her skin. The fact that he could make her laugh, and understood how she felt, on top of everything, made her attraction to him more dangerous.

She handed the near-empty glass back to him and he saluted her with it before backing out of the stall. The curtain closed snugly again, she somehow managed to wriggle out of the dress and kick off the heels, belatedly realizing she hadn't gone out for her next outfit.

As if he'd read her mind, Brendan cleared his throat seconds before slipping his big hand around the edges of the curtain. A hanger bearing a royal-blue gown dangled from one finger. The color of the dress, so rich it looked almost iridescent, instantly caught Rose's fancy.

His deep, smooth voice reached her through the curtain. "This is the one I'd pick if I were you."

"Thanks," Rose murmured, as she lifted the hanger from his finger and placed it on a hook. A jab of disappointment hit her when she realized that the long dress not only lacked sleeves, but straps, too.

She had never worn a strapless dress in her life. She'd never had a reason to. By the time she'd been old enough to go to the prom she'd already decided that if she never became involved with anyone she could never be hurt. But it couldn't hurt to try on the dress.

She took the dress down and unzipped the back.

Her heart started to beat a little faster at the beautiful color and how wonderful the substantial, silky fabric felt in her hands as she pulled the narrow gown up over her hips. As she slipped the fitted bodice over her breasts her jaw dropped in awe at how perfectly cut the dress was, how it molded her curves as if made for her. Telling herself she was simply curious, she unfastened her bra and took it off. The gown's straight neckline was surprisingly modest.

She reached behind her and pulled the zipper as high as she could, which wasn't all the way. No matter how she came at it, she couldn't zip up the dress completely.

She must have grunted, or something, because Brendan asked, "Is everything all right?" He was still standing just outside the stall, with only a curtain between them. Her vitals went through the roof. Where in the heck were the saleswomen?

"I can't zip it up all the way."

"I'll get it."

The brass curtain rings slid along the rod as Brendan invaded her space once again. Only this time she knew he was going to touch her. Her core temperature kicked up several more notches. Rose watched his reflection in the mirror, and he seemed intent on doing nothing more than zipping the dress the rest of the way up. The backs of his fingers barely brushed her skin, but goose bumps erupted all over her body with a delicious shiver.

He looked at her in the mirror. His warm hazel eyes widened, and his lips parted as his gaze traveled over her. Her heart palpitated like crazy in response.

His gaze met hers. "I was right. That's the one. That's the dress meant for you."

"It's not—" Her voice sounded raw with awareness, so she stopped and cleared her throat. "It's not what I was going for."

"Who cares? It's perfect." He took her hand in his and started backing out of the stall. "Come out here so you can get a better look."

She shook her head, leaning back to counter his gentle, steady pull. She didn't want to get a better look, because she couldn't buy it. She'd never avoid being noticed in this dress.

Brendan raised one eyebrow, silently questioning her resistance. She stonily refused to respond. She would not give him more ammunition to use against her, more tools in his bag of tricks to charm her.

His expression turned coaxing as he pulled a little harder on her hand. "Come take a quick look."

Her goal *had* been to get the ordeal over with quickly, and she had thus far failed miserably. Rose gave in, telling herself she'd look for expediency's sake. She allowed Brendan to lead her to the bay of mirrors. His grip on her hand loosened, becoming less controlling and more caressing. Something in his expression also shifted, and her skin responded with a hot flush before her brain had a chance to temper it with logic.

When they saw her all three saleswomen gasped. Clarice raised her hands as if her prayers had been answered. After a few seconds' silence they voiced their approval in a clamor of compliments.

Brendan ignored them as he steered Rose up onto the pedestal. She was too distracted by the feel of her hand in his and the hot look in his eyes to point out they weren't done yet. She wasn't buying this dress.

Brendan released her hand and nodded toward the mirrors. "See? It looks even better out here."

Rose caught sight of her reflection, and her mouth dropped open. The gown looked incredible on her— made *her* look incredible. Like someone else. The sleek bodice accented her breasts without drawing too much attention to them, and it molded her waist and hips into an hourglass shape, the rich fabric smooth along impeccably sewn seams.

She turned to the side and discovered the dress had a sort of flounce, or train, or whatever it was called, that began at the middle of her bottom and flowed out behind her just enough to give the gown an incredible air of romance.

Something Rose had purposefully never let herself experience before. *If she never went along for the ride, she couldn't be abandoned along the way.*

Clarice stepped onto the pedestal next to her. "And with her hair pulled back like this..." She gathered Rose's shoulder-length hair at the nape of her neck and deftly twisted it into a knot similar to her own, securing it with hairpins from her pocket.

"Coupled with matching shoes…" One of the other women produced a pair of pointy, high-heeled mules in the same incredible blue. Rose stepped into them, thinking they were the cutest shoes she'd ever seen.

Clarice sighed. "She is the epitome of elegance and sophistication."

Brendan quietly stated, "She looks like a princess."

Rose jerked her gaze to his in the mirror, but he was looking at her profile, not her reflection. Or her figure.

A princess. No one had ever in her entire life compared her to a princess.

Her foster parents had enjoyed reminding her and everyone else within earshot that she was "Little Lost Rose." Dr. Williams had always called her "Little Miss Determined." The other doctors and nurses at the hospital didn't realize she knew they called her "Dr. Doberman." And she'd always considered herself "Little Miss Nobody," because no one could tell her who she really was, where she'd come from.

But she'd never reminded anyone of a princess.

Whether she was being manipulated or not, pleasure spread through her like a narcotic. A drug that would leave her weaker once it left her system.

She remembered all too well the rush of excitement at getting a new family—only it hadn't lasted.

Brendan met her gaze in the mirror. She searched

his hazel eyes and handsome face, but couldn't find any trace of guile. What she did see was hard to decipher, but physical appreciation was definitely there. The corner of his mouth curled upward, his approval of her looks taking on decidedly sexual overtones.

The raw desire in his expression shook her to the core, releasing profound need inside her she'd never felt before. She was at a loss over how to deal with his reaction, or her own, so she did what she always did when she felt threatened or unsure: she bolted.

Slipping past Clarice, Rose stepped off the pedestal and headed toward the changing stall. "It's very nice, but as I said before, it's not what I had in mind." Expecting protests and feeling more than ready to finally put an end to this misadventure, she swallowed her earlier misgivings and added, "As a matter of fact, the first dress I tried on—the black one with wide straps—came the closest, though I really would have preferred sleeves. I think I'll buy that one."

Clarice shook her head. "Oh, no, no. That gown, while a wonderful dress by one of the finest designers, is a sack on you compared to this one. I have honestly never seen a woman so perfectly suited for a gown in my entire career."

Her eyes welling unexpectedly at the choice she had to make to blend in—as well as at refusing this feminine fantasy she would never have the courage to indulge in—Rose shut out Clarice and her argument with a jangling tug on the curtain.

Brendan murmured something, and Clarice didn't say any more.

Rose nearly dislocated her shoulder doing it, but she was able to unzip the back of the dress far enough to wriggle out. She pulled on her chinos, blouse and blazer, then crammed her feet back in her shoes as quickly as she could. Unable to bear seeing the beautiful dress crumpled up on the floor, she took the time to put it back on its hanger, though she probably did it wrong.

Her jaw set, she left the stall and was surprised to find the parlor empty. She went out into the main part of the store. Brendan was leaning casually on the tall counter hiding the register. He'd been watching the door to the changing area, his expression blank enough that Rose couldn't tell what he was thinking.

She reminded herself that what he thought didn't matter. She was doing this for the hospital, for Dylan, and it would only be for one evening.

Next to Brendan, one of the saleswomen was holding up the black gown Rose had decided to buy. Clarice and the other woman were standing behind the counter, obviously making an effort to keep their expressions neutral.

Brendan pointed at the black gown. "Is that the one?"

Rose nodded. "Yes. That's the one."

"And the shoes, too?" he asked.

"The shoes, too."

He nodded. "All right then." He reached into his pants pocket and pulled out a slender brown leather credit card holder and money clip. He slipped out a platinum credit card and held it toward Clarice. "Ring us up, please."

Rose nearly shouted, "No!" Everyone looked so startled that she forced a smile to soften her outburst. She dug in her pocket for her own little wallet. "I'll be paying for this." She refused to be in any way beholden to him.

It was bad enough being attracted to him in every way imaginable.

BRENDAN CONSIDERED insisting on paying for the gown because she only needed it to help him out with the fund-raiser, but he didn't think she'd been given the nickname "Dr. Doberman" for nothing. She was tenacious as hell. He seriously doubted she would relent.

Just as she hadn't entirely relented regarding the shopping trip. Yes, she was buying a lovely gown that made her look elegant and poised, but in the end she'd managed to walk out with one of the first dresses she'd tried on. Which he knew as well as he knew his name had been her goal all along.

Brendan smiled. She really was something.

He watched her studiously ignore him as she came up to the counter and handed over her credit card. The lead saleswoman shot him a glance, clearly having seen this sort of mating ritual played out before by wealthy men and their independent-minded but easily bought lady friends. Though he'd only known her a short time, Brendan felt the surest way to alienate Rose and lose her cooperation with the fund-raiser would be to play that sort of game with her now.

When he didn't tell Rose to put her credit card away, nor insist on paying for the gown himself, the saleswoman took Rose's card and swiped it through the machine. Rose flinched, and Brendan decided he'd find a way to reimburse her for the cost of the dress through Dr. Williams. It hadn't been her idea to buy a designer gown from an exclusive boutique. But his best donors would recognize a gown from this store in an instant, which would add considerably to her reliability quotient.

Despite her obvious concern about the cost, she signed the sales slip in a doctor's scrawl without a discernable glance at the total.

The admiration coupled with the horniness that had gripped him the second she'd closed the curtain to strip should have had him running for the hills. But repairing his reputation here in Chicago meant more to him than his need to stay away from women who could make him lose his focus again. Besides,

Rose wasn't the predatory type. Far from it. She looked more like a woman afraid of being hunted.

And he'd been on the prowl.

A growing urge to protect joined his admiration for her. Someone, somewhere, had done this gorgeous woman serious damage. He saw it in the shadow of uncertainty in her eyes, and in the way she shifted away from him when he got too close.

Too bad he had no intention of sticking around town long enough to find out who'd hurt her, because he'd pound the guy's face in. Just as he now had no intention of acting on the desire that had hit him like a truck when he'd seen her in the blue dress. A dress he'd known would look great on her tall, slender body. In a color that set off her remarkable hair, and made her blue eyes glow.

But if he'd had any idea of just how good she'd look, he might have reconsidered picking it out for her. There was no way he'd ever get the image of her in that dress out of his head. Not to mention the soul-lifting sound of her laughter, or the look on her face when he'd called her a princess. She deserved to feel like that again.

And he knew exactly how to make it happen.

Though it would be the ultimate test of his ability to stick to his plan of staying focused on repairing his reputation.

Chapter Six

Despite the dimness of the porch light, Rose spotted the large, flat box leaning against her front door as she pulled into her narrow driveway Thursday night. The package had to be the bedding and matching wall hanging she'd ordered from a catalog the week before. Pleasure energized her tired body as she pulled into the single-car garage tucked behind her house.

She'd planned to crawl into bed the second she arrived home, but adding welcoming touches to what she hoped would eventually be Dylan's room was better than sleep any day. Or night, considering it was well past ten. She'd come home from the hospital a little earlier than normal out of sheer exhaustion.

Her sleep had been disrupted yet again the night before by thoughts of a certain gentleman and memories of his electrifying touch, his heat-generating presence, his charm. All the things she'd been so determined not to be affected by. So much for determination.

After parking her car and closing up the garage, she entered the house through the back door, as usual. She flicked on the light in the small remodeled kitchen, the new stainless steel appliances still gleaming from lack of use. That would change as soon as she brought Dylan home. The thought warmed her as nothing else could.

Rose deposited her backpack and keys on the antique kitchen table before heading for the foyer. When she opened the front door, the package fell inward, top down, with a *thwack* on the hardwood floor. She squatted to pick it up, expecting it to be heavy with the weight of the bedding. But the large box was surprisingly light.

She took the package to the kitchen table and used the sharp tip of one of her keys to slice open the tape. The quilted hanging of a train would look great over the big-boy twin bed she'd already set up in the room across the hall from hers, and would be safe for Dylan to sleep beneath. She opened the cardboard flaps and paused, her weary brain taking a moment to realize the package contained a white plastic garment bag on a hanger secured on a cardboard loop.

Her heart beat hard as she pulled the hanger from the box. There was a shoebox beneath the garment bag.

The front of the bag bore the logo of the dress shop Brendan had taken her to the night before. It was exactly like the one already hanging in her bedroom closet, with the black dress she'd insisted on buying inside.

She unzipped the bag a little and caught a glimpse of rich, royal-blue fabric. Her hand stalled along with her breath. Draping the gown over a chair, she reached for the shoebox, discovering it contained the pair of matching pointy-toed, high-heeled mules. She tore through wadded tissue paper until she found a small vellum envelope embossed with the store's name. She opened the sealed flap, not surprised her hands were shaking.

This could be a mistake, or the result of some misunderstanding. But in the pit of her stomach she knew why this dress had been sent to her house.

And by whom.

The handwriting on the note was decidedly feminine, with a lot of loops and curls, but as she read the short message, her suspicions were confirmed.

''This dress was meant for you.''

She could hear Brendan's voice in her head, saying those words. She remembered what he'd said when he'd handed the gown through the curtain. *This is the one I'd pick if I were you.*

This was the dress he wanted her to wear tomorrow night to the auction. Taking refuge in anger, she clenched her jaw at his arrogance. Did he think he could get his way by sending her this dress? Was he foolish enough to believe he'd earn points by buying it for her?

She picked up the gown, intending to shove it in the box right away so she could send it back tomorrow. But the small amount of fabric she'd exposed glowed under the kitchen's overhead light. She stopped. Had Brendan really bought this dress and had it sent to her because he couldn't stand not to get his way? Or was it that he'd seen through her protests and excuses to how she really felt about it? How this gown had made her feel like the princess he'd compared her to?

Her stomach churned at the thought that she could be so transparent, and to Brendan L. MacDougal, of all people. But he had caught her in a weak moment the night they'd first met. Had that glimpse of vulnerability given him a window into the real Rose Doeber? A shiver of dread ran through her, even as she dismissed the idea. He couldn't have seen the real her, because no one—not even Rose—knew who that was.

No dress would change that.

She unzipped the garment bag completely and took the exquisite dress out. She couldn't imagine how much it must have cost Brendan, but considering how wealthy the MacDougals reportedly were, she supposed it was much like her buying him a T-shirt.

So perhaps the gesture didn't have as much significance to him as it would to someone of normal means. She rolled the idea around as she wandered down the hall to her bedroom, the blue gown held out in front of her. The faintly iridescent material carried a shimmer of light with it down the dim hall. She'd never owned anything so gorgeous in her life.

Wouldn't she be making a bigger deal out of his buying the dress if she made a show of refusing it? And despite the fact that he could certainly afford it, didn't he deserve to be out the price of the gown for being so presumptuous?

Turning on the bedroom light, she laughed softly and shook her head at her rationalizations. But it *was* a gorgeous dress, and she *did* look great in it.

Which was exactly why she couldn't wear it.

The look of appreciation in Brendan's eyes was still clear in her mind. As was her body's response to it. So much so she'd hardly slept last night, tossing and turning with what she had to admit was a sexual restlessness he'd awakened.

And she had spent the day glancing down the hospital corridors either hoping or fearing—she wasn't sure which—for a glimpse of Brendan among his brother's entourage. Her preoccupation with him was reason enough to put the dress away for good.

Her attraction to Brendan was cause for major concern, if attraction was the right word for the way her temperature spiked and her skin prickled at the thought of his hot hazel eyes and his deep, smooth voice.

She stood in front of the Victorian standing mirror she'd found at a flea market and held up the dress. If she wore this gown instead of the black one, would the attention she received be the least of her problems? Would she find it harder to resist Brendan's charm?

From her teens on, she'd lived her life believing that if she never went along for the ride, she couldn't be abandoned along the way. Which was why she'd never felt like a princess before. And why she needn't fear a little attraction. It wasn't as if she'd act on it.

She ran a hand down the blue material. Would it really hurt to be a princess for one night?

"I WAS ABOUT READY to have you paged," Brendan said with a lazy smile as Rose strode toward him across the hotel lobby's marble floor as quickly as her black dress and high heels would allow. She was gripping her dressy new purse so tightly she decided it should be called a *strangle* rather than a clutch. Barely two minutes had passed since she'd reassured herself she would have no trouble keeping a low profile tonight. After hours of soul searching she had decided that was more important to her than a night of fantasy.

Not that Brendan didn't look exactly like the fantasy he'd appeared to be the first time she'd seen him. He stood a good head taller than the other men in the lobby, and his shoulders looked impossibly broad beneath his tuxedo jacket, strong enough to handle any burden. If only she could unload hers on him.

Tonight his mahogany hair was smooth and unrumpled, and the compassion that had softened his expression when he'd found her crying had been replaced by speculative watchfulness. She'd worried how he'd react to her not wearing the blue dress, and although she was late she would have expected him to comment on that first, rather than her tardiness.

"I had a patient I didn't want to leave until some critical tests came back," she explained.

His dark brows slammed downward. "Dylan?" The concern in his voice was plain.

She shuddered at the thought. "No, not Dylan. An eight-year-old boy was trying to ride two scooters at once down a steep road."

Brendan winced. "Unsuccessfully, I take it."

"I guess he was doing pretty well until he ran into a parked car. Thank goodness for helmets."

Offering her his arm, he asked, "Is he going to be okay?"

She hesitated only a moment before slipping her hand beneath his arm and settling it lightly on his crooked elbow, forcing herself to focus on the conversation rather than the warmth and strength her hand encountered. They walked toward a burgundy-carpeted stairway that led to the mezzanine level.

There had to be something about Brendan in a tuxedo, because the magnetic pull of his body kept her close to his side.

She did her best to fight the unseen tug. "Yes. I couldn't find any sign of hemorrhage or swelling."

He returned the wave of a couple passing them. "I'm glad you took the time to make sure."

Her hard-earned suspiciousness flared. "Because now I won't be too preoccupied to be in a party mood?" She couldn't help her glacial tone.

He stopped and gazed at her, hazel eyes sharp with indignation. "Because kids deserve the extra care."

Rose swallowed, embarrassed by her assumption that he only cared about his fund-raising. He was so innately suited to the task, his charm and incredible presence so difficult to resist. But resist she would. Though adding a genuine concern about children to his growing list of attributes would make resisting even harder.

A question popped into her mind, one that she should have asked the day of the photo shoot. "Why do you do this?"

"Do what? Defend myself?"

She squeezed his arm and smiled before she could stop herself from responding to his mock indignation. "No. Why are you directly involved with the fund-raising for your family's foundation? I thought foundations usually hired people to administer their funds. Or is this a special case?"

His nostrils flared as he inhaled deeply. Glancing around, he led her out of the flow of elegantly dressed people ostensibly on their way to the auction. He found a spot near some large tinted windows overlooking the concrete banks of the canal. "Why would you think this is a special case?"

She shrugged. "Because two members of the MacDougal family, you and your brother, are so actively involved." A disturbing thought occurred to her. "You don't live in Chicago, do you?"

"No. And neither does Rory. My whole family lives in or around New York City. Although my oldest brother, Wilder, splits his time between New York and Oregon, where his wife's family lives."

As subtly as she could, Rose let out a relieved breath and looked out the window at a passing tour boat loaded with camera-wielding visitors, who were snapping shots of the tall buildings and endless bridges despite the failing light. After she fulfilled her part of the deal, she wouldn't have to see him again, wouldn't have to be tempted by his charming smile, his wit, his broad shoulders...

He turned back toward the increasing number of formally dressed couples moving past them. With a surprisingly stiff smile, he nodded a greeting to someone he obviously knew. "To answer your first question, as a matter of fact, I was hired. Sort of. Running the foundation is my job."

"Really? I figured that with a family like yours—"

"I'd be managing portfolios?" He shook his head. "My father and his brothers oversee the family's investments and business ventures. Well enough that my generation has been free to pursue other interests, if we want.

"In my immediate family, Wilder has his own mergers and acquisitions company. Rory, as you know, races cars. My sisters are the only ones interested in working directly with my father."

Rose couldn't fathom what belonging to a family such as his would be like and, for her own good, was unwilling to try. "Actually, I was going to say that I figured you didn't work at all. That you were more along the lines of a playboy."

He laughed. The deep, rich sound flowed through her, filling more than a few dark, lonely places. "Well, there's always time for that. But I love being able to make a difference in a big way, especially where children are concerned."

Rose's throat closed up. She wouldn't let him affect her. She wouldn't. But acquiring a complete understanding of the workings of the human brain would be easier.

Glancing at his watch, Brendan guided her to the

stairs. The cocktail reception and silent auction had probably already started. "Plus, I don't mind the social aspect of fund-raising."

"Now that doesn't surprise me."

He shot her a sidelong glance. "Oh, really?"

Unexpectedly warmed by the twinkle in his eye, she smiled. "Yes, really."

He gave her a playful wink and proved her right by hailing a couple on the stairs ahead of them. They returned his greeting but continued toward the mezzanine.

When they reached the top, Brendan returned his gaze to hers, focusing on her more intensely than he had since she'd arrived. "So, what about you? Did you escape a family business? Or are you following in the footsteps of a long line of doctors in your family?"

Fighting a swell of panic, Rose shook her head. "No, nothing like that. I just always wanted to be a doctor."

"Why pediatric neurology?"

She shrugged and tried for an offhand air. "I like a challenge."

"It would have been cheaper to take up golf."

She forced a laugh. Fearing he'd continue to press, and with nowhere she could bolt to, she offered him something substantial, and unfortunately true. "I knew Dr. Williams when I was growing up. Before he took over the entire pediatrics department, pediatric neurology was his specialty. He knew it would be perfect for me, and encouraged me to try it.''

''Really?'' The news obviously pleased Brendan. ''Was he friends with your parents?''

Bolting mentally if not physically, Rose looked through the open double doors into the large room full of people socializing. ''Shouldn't we be getting back to *your* specialty?''

It took him a moment, but he finally agreed. ''Yes, I suppose we'd better.'' He led her toward the couple he'd hailed on the stairs.

Self-conscious about having held on to him for so long, Rose released Brendan's arm, planning to hang back. He proceeded to catch her hand in his, grasping it with a gentle but firm grip. She had no choice but to meet the other couple when he promptly made the introductions, stressing her occupation and her reason for attending the evening's gathering.

At first the couple seemed disinclined to stop and chat. But when Brendan kept the focus on Rose and what she knew about the hospital's needs, they relented. Rose had no choice but to carry the conversation. It was the most she'd talked outside of work in ages, but since she was talking about work it wasn't difficult.

The rest of the cocktail reception and silent auction progressed in much the same way, with Brendan seeking people out as they wrote down bids for items—mostly bottles of wine—elaborately displayed on long tables throughout the room. He never failed to remember names or associations. Despite her determination to remain detached, Rose found herself admiring Brendan's dedication and the almost earnest way he spoke of the cause they were raising money for.

At first she thought she was imagining things, but the people Brendan appeared most eager to speak with seemed to be avoiding him. A few were downright cool.

One couple, a thin older man with a shiny bald head and his equally slender gray-haired wife, dressed in a long black gown with silver beading, turned away when Brendan and Rose approached. Their escape attempt was thwarted by the crowd near a table loaded with oversize wine bottles and baskets brimming with gourmet delicacies to be enjoyed on overnight getaways.

"Mr. and Mrs. Van Hoven!"

Rose noted that Brendan's greeting was loud and cheerful enough that it couldn't be tactfully ignored—though Mr. Van Hoven's hesitation made it clear he'd considered it. Mrs. Van Hoven raised her chin and flat-out glared at Brendan.

Stunned to discover that she clearly wasn't imagining things, that her escort's appeal wasn't universal, Rose glanced at Brendan. His handsome smile was firmly in place—so much so that Rose could see the strain of tension in his jaw and neck. She drew back her chin. What was going on?

Mr. Van Hoven made an exasperated sounding noise. "Brendan."

Brendan didn't extend his hand as he had to everyone else he'd greeted so far, adding fuel to Rose's curiosity.

Instead, he inclined his head slightly. "Thank you for coming tonight. I know what a busy schedule you have, sir. The presence of you and your lovely wife adds so much to this event."

Mrs. Van Hoven arched a thin brow. "Too bad the same can't be said about yours."

Rose blinked. The woman had just insulted Brendan L. MacDougal of the MacDougal Foundation MacDougals. Granted, Rose knew how wealthy and powerful his family was because of their generosity toward children's hospitals, but she had to believe this woman had also heard of them. To insult him at his own function called for either a perception of higher social status or a huge set of—

The thought was cut off when Brendan's grip on her hand tightened until it hurt. No one else would know that Mrs. Van Hoven's slam had had any affect on him, because his expression remained friendly. And while Rose burned with curiosity about what Brendan could have done to earn this sort of animosity, she knew a thing or two about hiding what she really felt, and gave a quick return squeeze of solidarity.

He acknowledged her gesture by instantly loosening his grip and running his thumb across the back of hers. The simple gesture made her throat close up again, this time with unexpected—not to mention unwanted—yearning.

He inclined his head to Mrs. Van Hoven once more. "Which is why I brought along the lovely Dr. Rose Doeber."

He finally looked at Rose, lifting her hand so he could tuck it into the crook of his arm again. The chandeliers were dimmed to the point that she couldn't make out what emotion his eyes might have held.

Covering her hand with his own, he continued, "Dr. Doeber is a pediatric neurologist at Chicago General and cares passionately for the children at the hospital. She can speak directly to any concerns you might have regarding the need for the pediatric wing expansion and the general upgrade to the facility."

The Van Hovens looked at her with blatant surprise. Long ago hardened to such reactions, she smiled and offered her hand. Mr. Van Hoven recovered his manners first and shook it. Mrs. Van Hoven, looking inexplicably wary, acknowledged Rose only by nodding.

Mr. Van Hoven eyed them both, then slowly

shook his head. "You've a deep hole to climb out of, Brendan. And for me, the jury's still out. Good evening." He nodded to Rose, then cupped his wife's elbow to lead her away.

After they left, Rose turned and raised her brows at Brendan and looked at him expectantly.

He ran a hand over his eyes. "I suppose there are some things you're going to have to know, after all."

Her shoulders tensed at the thought that he'd brought her into the middle of something without letting her in on what was going on. While she couldn't blame him for keeping secrets, when she had so many of her own, she did have a right to know what she was involved in.

She let go of his arm and pulled her hand from beneath his. "You *suppose?*"

He took her elbow the same way Mr. Van Hoven had taken his wife's, though Rose doubted the sour-faced Mrs. Van Hoven felt the same tingle, the same awareness, that she did.

Guiding her away from the auction tables, Brendan leaned in close and spoke softly. "You asked before if this fund-raising campaign was a special case."

Despite being bombarded by the spicy scent of his aftershave, the heat radiating from his big body, the seductiveness of his voice, she met his gaze. "Yes, I did."

He studied her for a moment, his eyes speculative, then looked at the couples and small groups moving past them, all chatting amiably. Steering her closer to the wall, he pulled in a deep breath. "Well, it is a special case. This is not the first time I've asked these people to give money to expand Chicago General's pediatric program."

Rose found it difficult to focus because of the aura of intimacy he'd unwittingly created. She frowned. "So? Sometimes it takes more than one event to raise enough—"

"I raised more than enough before. It was all stolen."

She gaped at him. "You're kidding. By whom?"

"A woman named Rebecca Crestfield. She passed herself off as a 'patron of the Windy City's poor.'"

"And they—" she waved a hand at the roomful of Chicago's most financially privileged "—blame you? Why?"

He looked away. "I released the money to her. It was my responsibility."

Rose set her jaw as her blood heated with indignation on Brendan's behalf. Having seen firsthand how hard he worked at communicating the importance of the pediatric wing and how great the need was for young patients, she was galled to see them snub him for someone else's actions. "Did you know she was a thief before you signed over the money?"

"No."

"Then how can they blame you?"

His eyes were shadowed by half-closed heavy lids. "As I said before, it was my responsibility."

"That's just wrong." It surprised her how strongly his predicament affected her. She told herself it was only because she cared about the children who might not receive the help they needed, cared about the improvements that wouldn't be made to the hospital because there wouldn't be enough money. It had nothing to do with the man in front of her pulsing with a frustration and self-recrimination that twisted something deep in her chest.

His velvety low voice called her back from her thoughts. "That's why I need your help."

"You've got it." Before she could think through what she suddenly felt compelled to do, she spun on one high heel and headed for the couple she suspected were the most influential in the room.

"Mr. and Mrs. Van Hoven." Rose interrupted the conversation they were having with a jewel-encrusted woman she hadn't met yet. "Excuse me, but I really would like to speak to you regarding how your opinion of Brendan MacDougal is directly affecting the welfare of the children served by Chicago General." She gained the undivided attention of not only the Van Hovens and the woman with them, but conversations all around them ceased.

Rose continued, despite the attention she was drawing. She couldn't stop herself from defending Brendan. "Obviously, I've made those kids my life. I have no choice but to care about them with every bone in my body. For Brendan MacDougal, however, it is a choice. A choice that has clearly cost him—unfairly, I might add. But he hasn't turned his back on those children. Neither should you."

She paused significantly, daring to look each and every one of them in the eye. "Those kids need what your donations can give them. Please don't forget that crucial point."

The fact that a substantial crowd of undoubtedly very important people were staring at her sank in, and heat exploded in Rose's cheeks. She mumbled some sort of goodbye, and turned to make a hasty retreat.

Only to slam into Brendan's broad chest. He caught her by the shoulders and steadied her, his hands warm and gentle.

Behind her, Mr. Van Hoven chuckled. "Seems you have a champion, Brendan. Here's hoping you know a little more about her than the last one."

Chapter Seven

Brendan stood on the curb of the hotel's circular drive, waiting with Rose for her car to be brought around. He couldn't shake Van Hoven's parting salvo.

Here's hoping you know a little more about her than the last one.

His gut twisted. Despite Terence's assurances, should Brendan have looked into Dr. Rose Doeber's background—or at least found out a little more about her—before presenting her more or less as his partner? He glanced at the woman standing next to him, clutching her little black purse to her chest like a shield. Her beautiful face revealed nothing, but she'd been stiff as a board since hearing Van Hoven's remarks.

Brendan had seen the flash of distress in her expression. Did she have something to hide?

No. The only thing she had to hide was her lack of experience at events such as this. He'd seen the way she'd surreptitiously watched the other women seated at their table, waiting for one of them to reach for a glass or utensil before she did, clearly uncertain whether to start on the right or left or when it was appropriate to begin eating.

And once she'd spent her glorious temper, she'd retreated into the cool shell he'd had to coax her out of earlier. She'd been incredible telling off the Van Hovens, conveying her passion without sacrificing her dignity. Standing up for him had been the very last thing he'd expected her to do. Whether he needed it or not, it made him feel very, very good to be defended by a woman like Rose.

His lack of knowledge about her became all the more worrisome, even with his heartfelt belief nothing unsavory lurked in her background or in her plans for the future. Was he making the same mistake again?

He'd thought it had been great to have Rebecca on his side, but that was nothing compared to having Rose's support. The intensity of the feeling probably came from knowing she didn't want to draw attention to herself—her choice of dress proof enough for him, yet she'd done it anyway by taking on the Van Hovens.

To make sure, Brendan gently asked, "Why didn't you wear the blue dress?"

She glanced at him, her equally blue eyes wide and bright with what looked like guilt. Then she looked away, and finally shrugged. "It was too revealing."

"Mmm." Maybe he knew more about her than he thought.

Though strapless, leaving her smooth arms and shoulders exposed, the blue gown had definitely been modest. But perhaps it had revealed something other than her tempting skin. He vividly remembered the shocked look on her face that had gradually given way to wonder when she'd seen how she looked wearing it. And how she'd shut it all down.

He suspected she hadn't worn that particular dress because she hadn't wanted anyone to see how gorgeous she really was. If that didn't make her a mystery, he didn't know what did.

Whether she ever wore it or not, he didn't want her to forget what was possible, how beautiful she was. "I made sure the store won't accept the dress if you try to take it back, you know."

She looked at him again, searching his face. "Why?"

"Because you should have it."

"But—"

"I want you to have that dress, Rose. Humor me."

She opened and closed her mouth, obviously unable to come up with an argument. "Fine."

One of the cars being brought around by the valets caught her attention, and she let out a breath of surrender. She pointed at the old white BMW. "This is mine."

Brendan felt encouraged by her capitulation, not to mention her choice of vehicles. It was not the car of a woman on the make—not flashy enough—nor was it the beater a woman in desperate straights would drive. Van Hoven's warning sounded in his head yet again.

Here's hoping you know a little more about her than the last one.

He mentally ticked off what he did know about Rose. She was a doctor working toward a specialization in pediatric neurology. Beautiful and poised despite a passion seething just below the surface. Dedicated. Stubborn. Beautiful. Intriguing. Beautiful. Mysterious.

Damn. He really didn't know enough about her. While it might very well be too late, especially since she'd already met his most influential donors, Brendan realized he needed to find out more about Dr. Rose Doeber. Her name was now attached to his.

As he watched the valet get out of her car, Brendan thought of one sure way to learn more about her. A visit to her home, where she spent her time away from work, might reveal a thing or two about her. She might also feel comfortable enough to open up to him about why she so desperately wanted to avoid notice.

Maybe he'd learn enough that he could give in to

the desire that had ricocheted through him like a bolt of lightning when she'd collided with him after giving old Van Hoven what for. Having her pressed into him, her breasts soft against his chest, his hands a perfect fit for the curve of her waist where he'd caught her to steady her had relit the fire she'd ignited at the dress boutique.

Most of all, he didn't want his evening with her to end just yet. He wasn't willing to consider why.

When the valet handed Brendan her car keys despite the fact she had her hand out for them, Brendan drew her behind a nearby column, out of sight of the other people waiting for their cars. "Can I drive you home?"

"No!" she blurted out.

He raised his eyebrows, surprised by the strength and speed of her refusal. And incredibly relieved by it. Rebecca sure as hell hadn't told him no. Just as she hadn't told him the truth.

Color flooded Rose's cheeks, giving her flawless fair skin a sexy flush. "I mean—that is, how will you get home then?" she stammered.

He shrugged, putting on a casual air that would hopefully change her mind. "Same way I'd get back to where I'm staying from here. Call my driver and have him pick me up."

She waved a dismissive hand, but wasn't as skilled at appearing casual as he was. The fact that she clearly didn't have much practice at the game of nonchalance was a very good sign.

As was the way her eyes kept darting to his mouth.

She licked her lips, driving all thoughts of casualness or information-gathering from his mind. "That's okay," she said. "I don't think I drank even a full glass of wine with dinner, so I'm fine to drive. But thank you, anyway."

He shifted toward her, pulled by the moisture shining on her full lower lip in the bright light of the hotel entrance. Drawing on what little he *did* know of her, he decided honesty was the best policy. Just look what telling her about Rebecca—at least part of the truth—had gained him: her support. "I'm not playing designated driver here."

Her gaze jumped from his mouth to his eyes, and her eyelids flared. "Then what are you playing at?"

She must not trust her ability to read men if she needed clarification. Another good sign. He reached up and tucked a silky blond strand behind a delicate ear. He was surprised by how much the minimal contact made him want to bury his whole hand in her incredible hair. "What am I playing at? This."

He lowered his head and kissed her.

He'd meant to keep the contact light and quick. But the second his mouth touched hers, discovering her lips to be as soft and yielding as he'd hoped they would be, every one of his good intentions was blasted to smithereens by the force of his desire for her. Only her squeak of surprise kept him from slanting his mouth against hers and delving deep.

He broke off the kiss and lifted his head.

She blinked wide eyes at him. "And what—" Her voice cracked, and she stopped to clear her throat. "What was that?"

"Nothing other than a guy who is grateful for the support of an incredible, beautiful woman, and isn't ready to say good-night to her and end their date yet."

"This—" She had to clear her throat again.

The idea that he was having an effect on her ratcheted his temperature up to the point he no longer cared if he learned anything about her other than how well her legs fit around his waist.

"This wasn't a date."

Her tenacity made him smile. "It can be."

She shook her head with an air of desperation. "No, it can't."

Wanting to change her mind, not upset her, he tried a more understanding tone. "Why not?"

"Because it shouldn't be. You're just here for this fund-raising campaign, which wraps up tonight, right?"

"Right." He hoped it proved successful. He *needed* it to be successful.

She pressed her pretty mouth flat before asking, "Then you're going back to New York?"

"So the fact that I don't live in Chicago is the problem?"

She gave a short, sarcastic laugh. "Actually, that's the one good thing."

Surprised at how stung he felt, Brendan shifted away from her. "I take it you simply don't want any sort of relationship with me."

"I don't want a relationship with anyone."

So it wasn't personal. He could work with that. *Keep it physical.* "Perfect. Neither do I. So let me come home with you."

ROSE COULD HARDLY THINK with her heart pumping blood through her veins as if she'd been given a shot of epinephrine. Brendan's kiss had sent her natural adrenaline level through the roof. His proposition had nearly given her a coronary.

He wanted to come home with her.

And he didn't want a relationship.

She should be offended. Instead, her mind started whirling with possibilities.

Earlier, Mr. Van Hoven's comment about hoping Brendan knew her better "than the last one" had almost made her turn tail and run. She didn't want anyone to know much of anything about her. Especially Brendan, with his prominent family and—thanks to Dr. Williams—his notion that she'd been on the donor side of charities.

But if Brendan didn't want a relationship, he didn't want to know more about her, right?

He just wanted to come home with her.

She needed to be clear about what he wanted. "So are you thinking a nightcap in front of a roaring fire? Because we'd have to stop by a liquor store—which aren't open this late—and someplace that sells pressed logs. Or are you proposing a one-night stand?"

He shrugged, but a corner of his wicked mouth curled up. "My schedule's pretty flexible the entire weekend...."

She started to comment on his cavalier attitude, but the thought of spending an entire weekend doing nothing but romping in the sheets with this guy made her forget what she was going to say.

He reached above her head and put a hand on the column behind her, leaning against it, crowding her space as effectively as her pounding heart was crowding her lungs. "And I don't believe the two are mutually exclusive."

Mostly to remind herself, she said as loudly as she dared, "Now, we're just talking sex here, not establishing a relationship that would lead to anything serious, right? A couple of times in the past I've made it very clear that I wanted to keep the two separate, but the guys ended up wanting more." Not entirely surprising, because she'd never been attracted to the type of man who wanted only sex.

And because she was more attracted to Brendan than she'd ever been to anyone, she couldn't completely trust his offer.

"Imagine that," he said dryly.

"So…well…"

"How about we just see how it goes. If you decide you want me gone, I'll be outta there." He reached into his breast pocket and pulled out a tiny cell phone. "I'll call the driver now and give him your address. I'll have him wait out front."

Her horror at the thought of some strange man waiting outside her house while she got it on with Brendan must have shown on her face, because he winced endearingly and quickly amended, "Or around the block?"

She shook her head adamantly. "No. Absolutely not."

He lowered his chin and his voice in the sexiest way. "No to the driver waiting, or no to—me?"

Rose closed her eyes against his handsome allure, but she couldn't shut out his animal heat, or the way his spicy scent stirred to life a gnawing hunger deep in the pit of her stomach.

This could very well be the last time she'd see him. Tomorrow he'd be gone from her life, and once again she'd be completely safe, on the path she'd chosen. But would she wonder forever what Brendan's strong arms felt like? What places he could have taken her with his big body, his sensuous mouth?

There were already so many unknowns in her life, so many things she would always be in the dark about. Was she willing to add one more?

She opened her eyes and met his gaze, sharp-edged with a blatant desire to get what he wanted.

He wanted her.

Yearning took hold of her with an unmerciful grip. Being wanted was the headiest drug for Rose. One she rarely had the chance to dabble in thanks to the hard, protective shell she'd developed over the years. But this man was offering it up to her on the cheap. All she had to do was want him back for the night. Maybe the weekend.

Then he'd be gone.

And she'd be left with a memory. Another thing most precious to her.

Her decision made, Rose let herself tumble into the hot caramel of his eyes. "Yes," she whispered.

Brendan's smile was slow, and very, very wicked.

As far as she was concerned, foreplay was over.

He leaned down and placed his mouth near her ear, his warm breath giving her nerve endings fits all over her body. "Yes, you're saying no to me? Or yes, you're saying no to the driver? Or yes—" he kissed her ear lightly "—you're saying…*yes?*"

Rose let loose a shudder of pleasure she could no longer contain, then stepped away from him, more than ready for them to be on their way. It was obvious from his smile he knew exactly what she'd meant. "Do you want to come home with me or not?"

He answered by taking her elbow and guiding her to the passenger door of her car. "Please say you don't live far away."

As he opened the car door for her, she said, "Why don't I just drive?"

"No way. I need to keep my hands occupied so I don't get us into a wreck."

Rose slipped into the passenger seat. The image of Brendan's hands on her body was clear enough in her head that her skin responded with a flush, banishing the chill in the spring air.

Brendan shut her door and rounded the car quickly, as if worried she'd change her mind. She saw him glance over his shoulder at the other guests waiting for their cars, and his expression sobered. Maybe he was more concerned about being seen leaving with her.

Why it would matter was beyond her. They'd been pretty much joined at the hip the entire evening. Little wonder she was so hot and bothered. While tonight hadn't started out as a date, it was certainly ending up that way.

Her pulse started racing again when he climbed into her car, filling it with what she considered his essential elements: heat, a heady scent and a sexual presence that robbed her brain of oxygen. So much so that she didn't think to object when he changed every single seat and steering wheel setting—settings that had taken her days to get just right.

At least she had the presence of mind to ask weakly, "Do you have protection? I don't, so if you don't we'll have to stop—"

He halted in the middle of moving his seat back, and gave her an almost censuring look. "You have to ask, after seeing the look on my face when you tried on that blue dress?"

Torn between feeling flattered and insulted that he'd planned to proposition her, Rose couldn't think of a response.

He chuckled. "Well, now I know how to leave you speechless. I was just kidding. Actually, we'll have to make a quick stop at a convenience store."

Rose nodded, relieved he wasn't playing her.

After he had the driver's seat adjusted to his liking, he started the car and pulled out of the hotel's circular drive without asking her which direction to turn. That he turned the right way unnerved her.

"How do you know which way to go?"

"I'm guessing. Well, no I'm not, actually. A woman as dedicated to her work as you are lives somewhere in the vicinity of said work. I figured that if I headed toward the hospital, I'd be heading in the right direction." He glanced at her. "So did I figure right?"

Rose shifted in her seat. His uncanny ability to read her was not a good thing. "Yes. Sort of. I used to live in a studio apartment only a block and a half from the hospital."

"Used to?"

She was uncertain how much of her life to reveal, despite being on her way to revealing all to him physically. She only offered, "I recently moved into a house. But it's not all that far from the hospital. You're still going in the right direction."

"Good. The last thing I want to do is to make a wrong turn with you, Doctor."

Her well-used defenses rose up at his double meaning. After the princess comment, she'd thought he viewed her differently from the people she'd worked with at the hospital. Which, she supposed, was the only reason she'd allowed him in her car. "Why do you say that?"

He took a hand from the wheel and placed it on her knee. The damp heat of his palm went straight through her gown and panty hose and hit deep tissue. "Because I have a feeling you haven't been given exactly what you really, truly want in a very long time. I don't want you disappointed in any way tonight, Rose."

His words, delivered in his incredibly smooth, deeply seductive voice, melted her on the spot. All she could say was, "Oh. Okay."

He shot her a grin, then returned his gaze to the

busy streets as they made their way across town. His attention wasn't entirely on driving, though. His hand slowly made its way up her leg, stroking and kneading, the skirt of her long gown bunching in his path.

As he followed her directions home—and he turned out to be very good at that—she kept expecting him to slip his hand farther, deeper. But he didn't. The longer he didn't, the more she wanted him to. The more she wanted *him.* By the time they pulled into the parking lot of a convenience store near her house, she was ready to climb onto his lap.

All from a touch on her inner thigh.

As he made the quick trip in and out of the store, she told herself her need had less to do with his power over her—she refused to accept that he held any—and more to do with her lack of sexual encounters since starting her fellowship a year and a half ago. Things had been quiet during her residency. And most of her internship. The fact was, it had been a very long time since she'd been physically involved with anyone.

She just needed to take the edge off. That was all. Which meant she'd have no trouble keeping what she did with Brendan tonight physical. Her emotions wouldn't get involved.

To prove it, the second he took the key from the ignition after parking in her garage, she unbuckled her seat belt and leaned toward him. She caught his strong jaw in her hands, assaulted by the warmth of his skin and the contrast between the roughness of his emerging stubble and the smoothness of the skin above his beard line. She held him still so she could capture his lips with hers.

His mouth instantly molded to hers, but he continued to take his cue from her, to let her be in control. Rose had never felt anything so heady in her life. Or so reassuring. She *could* let this man into her relentlessly guarded world for one night.

She broke off the kiss and sat back, panting as if she'd just run for a code blue. ''We'd better go in now.''

He exhaled shakily and shook his head, as if to clear it. ''Wow. Either that or we're going to end up with a quickie in the car.''

Rose instantly imagined herself climbing onto his lap, her legs straddling his hips. While he'd be the one sitting in the driver's seat, she'd definitely be the one doing the driving. The thought was very tempting. There'd been far too many times when she hadn't been in control of her life. She caught her lower lip between her teeth and considered the space between his chest and the steering wheel.

He waved her off. ''No, no. That wouldn't fit with my plan to give you what you deserve tonight.''

The sense of power he gave her swelled within her chest, until she was damn near giddy and more than a little inclined to tease. In what she hoped would be a sultry voice, she countered, "I thought you were going to give me what I *want,* not what I deserve."

He eyed her, and while the dimness of the garage obscured his expression, her skin tingled beneath the heat of his gaze. His straight white teeth glowed from a naughty grin. His seat belt clicked when he unfastened it, and the whir of the electric seat motor startled her as his seat moved back. "You're right. I did." He reached out and slipped a big, warm hand into her hair. "Come here."

Adrenaline surged through Rose again. She yanked what seemed like yards of black dress material up around her thighs so she could climb over the console and onto his lap. One high heel caught on the steering wheel and her knee wedged painfully against the seat belt buckle. But the second she settled against the hot hardness filling his pants, nothing else mattered. Nothing except getting as close to this man as she possibly could.

He kissed her, delving deep into her mouth to find her tongue and flexing his hand against her scalp, but she set the pace. She was in control.

For all of two seconds.

He moved his hands downward, skimming her breasts enough to electrify them, then gripped her bottom to intensify the already almost unbearable contact. Rose's body took control. A ravenous need swamped her, sweeping her beyond the safe boundaries she'd always set for herself. Scaring her. She rationalized that since it was only for one night, everything would be okay. She'd still be safe. After he was gone.

Brendan's mouth, his tongue, his hands, kept pace with her, fueling the fire between them with a raging heat of his own. She rocked against him, pressing into him by arching her back. He slipped his hands toward her heat, but her panty hose kept him from touching her where he'd intended.

He broke off the kiss. "These things have *got* to go." His hands searched for the waistband.

Brought partway back to earth by how unsexy her control-top Lycra-blend nylons were, Rose inwardly cringed. He was probably used to women who only wore expensive matched underwear sets complete with bowed garters and seamed stockings. Rose based her undergarment choices on durability. The less often she had to shop for new ones, the better.

And she couldn't think of anything less sexy than the way she'd look trying to wriggle out of panty hose in the front seat of her car. "Maybe we should go inside, after all."

He gripped her hips and moved her against him. "Inside. Yes. Inside is good."

Her body reacted as if he'd touched her deep within. But he never would unless she lost the Lycra. It was time to go into the house.

She reached for the door handle and opened the

driver's-side door, freeing her trapped leg. She would have tumbled off his lap if he hadn't had her anchored there so firmly. So wonderfully. But she didn't doubt for a second that what he was currently making her feel would only get better once they made it to her bed.

With the skirt of her gown practically up around her waist, she didn't earn any style points as she climbed off his lap. The way his hand slid along her leg as she stepped out of the car made her not care.

Once her dress was back the way it was supposed to be, she snagged his hand and pulled as if they'd always been intimate. "Then come on."

Brendan climbed from her car, the look in his eyes as hot and strong as his grip. The creases in his tuxedo where she'd been straddling him cast deep shadows in the car's dome light. She blushed.

She'd always been plenty aggressive when it came to the welfare of her patients, who were too young and trusting to speak up for themselves. What people had called her "Doberman" tendencies also kept others from wanting to get too close.

But she'd never been this sexually aggressive before. For her to be this way with a man of Brendan's sheer presence amazed her, scaring her as much as her need for him.

She'd made her decision, though, and willed her fear away. She wanted Brendan. She wanted this memory with him. There was too big a void in her life where memories were concerned.

After he closed the car door, she led him from the garage, incredibly aware of how big his hand was grasping hers. On their way to the back porch, his thumb kept up a steady stroking. The motion reassured her, even when he crowded her against the door and his heat and spicy scent engulfed her. He put the key he'd picked as the best match into the lock.

The dead bolt clicked loudly. Lucky guess. He smiled as if there were very few locks he couldn't open.

Thank goodness he would never have any luck opening the lock on her heart.

Chapter Eight

The bite of the night air should have been enough to cool Brendan's jets, but he still had to force himself to focus on getting into the house. His body would have been more than happy to flatten Rose against the door and go at it right there.

When she'd rucked up her dress and climbed onto his lap, she'd cranked him up to a point he hadn't reached since his first sure thing. There was an intensity to her that he instinctively knew was going to blow his mind, and he couldn't wait to get busy with her.

But he was at her house for more than a good time. He was there to learn what he could about Dr. Rose Doeber, to reassure himself that he hadn't made the same mistake twice. To see if he could trust her.

His gaze drifted to her kiss-swollen lips as he turned the door handle. The woman certainly had a way of making him lose his focus. Hopefully that wouldn't turn out to be a bad thing.

He opened the door for her but didn't step out of the way, enjoying the brush of her bare shoulder against his chest and the chaos-inciting way she dragged a hand across his thighs as she stepped past him.

She flicked on a light and he followed her into what turned out to be a small kitchen, in line with what he would have expected from a quaint older home. Thanks to the buzzing heat her touch had left in its wake and the tantalizing sway of her hips beneath her black gown, the shining white tile and stainless steel appliances made only a vague impression on him as he trailed after her, a hound dog on a scent. His vision narrowed and every sense honed in on Rose.

Deciding the dark wood dinette table just beyond the kitchen would serve fine as a prop for her delectable bottom while they *talked*, Brendan reached for Rose as he rounded a corner. Before he had a chance to make contact, he stubbed his foot on a large cardboard box leaning against the wall. He nearly went head over keyster. Something in the box tinkled musically.

Rose stopped at the noise. She looked from him regaining his balance to the box, and immediately moved to shove what looked to be a mail-order package out of his way. "Oh, I'm sorry about that. I shouldn't have left this here. Are you all right?"

"Yeah, I'm fine." His first thought was that he'd tripped on the box containing the blue dress, but the dress couldn't have jingled. The kind of music he associated with baby toys had definitely come from within the big box. Maybe it was something for her work. Curious, he squinted at the shipping label. "What's in there?"

She practically jumped in front of him, blocking his view. "It's nothing."

The sexy, languid look was gone from her big blue eyes and she was clasping and unclasping her hands in front of her. As a matter of fact, she looked much as she had the first time he'd met her and had started asking questions about Dylan.

An unwanted suspicion cooled his blood in a way nothing else could. Why was she always so tight-lipped—except when it came to kissing? The suspicion sparked an unexpected burn of anger in the pit of his stomach. She had secrets; he had the need to know them.

He nodded at the box behind her. "That's an awfully jingly sounding nothing."

She glanced back at it and shifted on her feet. "It's, uh, it's a wind chime."

Man, was she a rotten liar. "Mmm. Must be a big one. And unique. I've never heard one that sounded like a baby toy before."

He saw her swallow hard and blink away what almost looked like fear. The muscles in his chest contracted and his ire melted. Shifting toward her, he slipped a hand beneath her hair and cupped the side of her neck, gently massaging the tightness he could feel there. "I'm not on the hospital's ethics board, Rose. It's okay to admit you buy things for your patients. Only a dunce wouldn't see how much you care for them. Dylan, in particular. It's one of the things I really like about you."

Her eyes widened a fraction, brightly reflecting what light made it around the corner from the kitchen. Then her gaze darted to a spot behind him before returning to meet his. Brendan automatically turned to see what she'd looked at.

Another, smaller box sat against the far wall, only this one had been opened. A royal-blue booster chair, the protective plastic pulled away, sat in front of it. Not exactly something a kid in a hospital would need.

Brendan remembered what she'd said when he'd found her crying over Dylan.

That's just it, he's not my son.

And the significance of her question: *You wouldn't happen to be a family court judge, would you?* hit him between the eyes.

Stunned, he met her gaze again. "Are you trying to gain custody of Dylan?"

Beneath his hand, the muscles in her throat worked, but she just stared at him.

He raised his other hand to cup her jaw. He could tell her teeth were clenched. "Why won't you confide in me, Rose? Why can't you let me inside your life? Even just a little." The force of his need to know surprised him—he was helpless against it.

Her eyes closed and she relaxed a little beneath his hands, but she shook her head, denying him.

Stung, he released her, blowing out a breath. "It all makes sense, now. Your possessiveness of Dylan, your unwillingness to have him used in a publicity campaign." Irrational anger seizing him again, he pointed at her. "You didn't want him in the campaign because you don't want any competition."

Her eyes flew open and she frowned fiercely. "No. That's not why at all. I'm all ready to start the process of adopting him, but—" She stopped herself and took a shuddering breath that made Brendan want to gather her into his arms despite his anger and frustration. Then she straightened into what he was starting to think of as her Dr. Doberman pose, the one that screamed, *Back off.* "I think it's time for you to call your driver."

Not only was she shutting him out, she was kicking him out.

He refused to give up that easily. "No. No way." He challenged her wall of secretiveness by crowding her space, reminding her where they had been heading with a brush of his chest and the touch of his hand on her jaw.

If she'd been willing to be physical with him, why wasn't she willing to tell him about her life? "Not until I get some answers." Their bargain sprang to mind and how protective she was of Dylan, how concerned she'd been about the photos. "For starters, why is it so important the photos of Dylan and Rory are only used locally?"

She searched his face as if she expected to find some sort of threat there. Then she caved, her body softening against his and her face nuzzling into his hand. "I have a good reason, Brendan. Really, I do."

His own body having no trouble at all remembering where they'd left off, he leaned down to kiss the corner of her mouth. "Just tell me, Rose. Trust me." He needed her to trust him in a way that had nothing to do with his desire for information. He did his damnedest to put a mental cork in it before the true reasons had a chance to seep into his consciousness.

Her hands slipped beneath his tux jacket to grip his sides. "I can't allow Dylan to be used in a national campaign because his father might see it."

Brendan pulled his chin back. "His father? I just assumed—"

"Bobby Ray's in Folsom Prison, serving a life sentence for being an accessory to murder during a drug deal gone bad. Though he should be doing time for hooking Dylan's mother on the same drugs, then leaving her to die because of them.'' Her tone held an older, fully matured version of the bitterness and contempt stirring in him.

''If he's in for life, how can it matter if he sees Dylan in a charity campaign?''

''He hasn't signed over his parental rights yet. When Dylan's mother died, they asked him if he wanted any part in Dylan's life. He didn't. Never had. But he's getting his kicks out of dragging things out. I imagine it's some sort of power trip.''

She closed her eyes and slowly shook her head. ''If he saw Dylan in photos with a famous race car driver, of all people, he'd never give up his rights. He'd never let me adopt Dylan if he thought Dylan could get him publicity of some kind.''

Brendan's insides twisted at her obvious fear. He slid his hands up into her hair and tried to reassure her. ''Come on now, Rory isn't that big of a deal.''

She relaxed against Brendan, pressing her forehead to his chin. ''He's a NASCAR driver, Brendan. I guarantee that's a big deal, especially to a guy like Bobby Ray.''

''But the odds of him actually seeing a charity campaign photo are next to nil. We make a concerted effort to reach only our target market, and believe me when I say Bobby Ray ain't it. Besides, I'm in charge, and I can promise you there's no way for him to benefit from Dylan's involvement. It's not going to happen.''

Brendan gently tilted her head back so he could look her in the eye, hoping she'd see his conviction. ''You got yourself worked up over nothing, sweetheart. No one is going to take Dylan away from you.''

''He's not mine yet.''

Brendan dropped a gentle kiss on her lush lips. ''But he will be.''

''If Bobby Ray signs the papers.'' Rose buried her face against Brendan's neck, wrapping her arms around his middle and holding on tight. ''I've never wanted anything so badly in my life, Brendan. I want to be there for Dylan, as his mom, always and forever. To love him and hold him and comfort him when he's scared. He deserves it.

''I bought this house, my car, this stuff—'' she nudged the big box with the side of her foot and set whatever was inside jingling ''—all for him. For the life we'll have together. Just the two of us.''

Just the two of us. No father, no husband, yet still a family of her own making. She'd really meant it when she'd said she wasn't interested in having the regular sort of relationship with him.

Brendan lowered his hands to gently stroke her back. ''What's in that box, anyway?''

''It's bedding, a quilted wall hanging and a matching night-light that fastens to a headboard.

When you touch it or, apparently, jostle it, music plays. I might have to rethink putting it on his bed, though, if it's that sensitive. I don't want it jingling every time he rolls over."

"We could always test it, you know."

She pulled away from him enough to raise her sleek, delicately arched eyebrows at him.

He gripped her narrow waist and shrugged, but couldn't squelch the grin pulling at his mouth. "Put it on your bed, see if it goes off." ·

"Like when the bed moves?"

"Yeah. When the bed moves."

She grimaced, but laughed. "I don't think so."

"Okay, bad idea. The night-light part, not the bed moving part, right?" He didn't wait for her answer. With the gentlest of pressure on her waist he started moving her backward toward what looked to be the hall to the bedrooms. Despite her revelations he hadn't forgotten or changed his mind about what they'd come here to do. He surprised himself a little by wanting her more now that he knew the depth of her character.

Best of all, a woman bent on adopting a child would do nothing to risk her reputation, let alone his. And if she was far enough along in the process to be outfitting her house for the child's arrival, there must not be anything in her past that could do damage to his family's foundation.

Not to mention the fact that she didn't want to be

anything more than physically involved. He raised his eyebrows at having actually found a woman he could have a truly risk-free relationship with.

She ran her hands up his back, her short fingernails making spine-tingling tracks through his shirt. "Right. Not the bed moving part."

Brendan's blood surged. Damn, he loved it when things went his way.

ROSE HAD NEVER IMAGINED it could be such a good thing to not be able to feel her feet. She knew they still worked, because she and Brendan were making steady progress toward her bedroom, but her brain seemed to refuse to acknowledge input from any part of her body other than those in direct contact with the man in her arms. Or the parts that wanted to be. There was no denying the signals coming from deep within her pelvis. She'd never wanted a man more in her life.

Nor had she ever shared so much about herself, revealed so much, without being swamped with remorse and paranoia. But telling Brendan about her plans to adopt Dylan, about her fears regarding Bobby Ray, felt right. It was a strange relief to unburden herself with him, if only for a moment. She would never have dreamed she would feel so good after taking such a risk.

Brendan gave her reason to hope. For what, she refused to consider.

He bent and kissed her where her jaw met her neck, a spot she hadn't known was so sensitive. The thinking part of her brain shut down completely. For once in her life she wanted to do nothing more than feel. No guarding, no suspicions. Because Brendan cared about the hospital and the children, because she'd been able to tell him about Dylan, because he was leaving, she could allow herself simple physical release.

They reached the door to her bedroom and turned to go in. Brendan paused long enough to hit the hall light switch with his elbow, providing enough light into her room to see by. Thankfully not enough to be embarrassed by. She backed into the room, kept on her feet by the grip she had on his strong, wide back and the steadying hold of his big, hot hands on her waist.

The way he swirled his tongue over the pulse points he unerringly found on her neck made her knees weak and her core turn liquid.

Barely two shuffling steps into the bedroom he slowly turned her around until her back was to him. Her bottom made firm contact with his hardness, and it was the most erotic thing she'd ever felt. Sparks flew every which way throughout her body.

His mouth against her ear, he said, "You are so beautiful, Rose. So damn beautiful." His deep, smooth voice was as compelling and seductive as she'd imagined it would be in the dark, washing over her as his fingers found the zipper on her dress and lowered it. The fact that he seemed to be cursing her for her beauty made his compliment more believable, less the meaningless platitude of a lover.

The fact that he was about to be her lover made her shudder in pleasure more than his warm breath on her ear or the touch of cool air on her newly exposed flesh. With her eyes fully adjusted to the room's dim light, she watched him guide the black fabric down her arms, his tan skin nearly as dark as her gown against her fair skin.

The heat and surprising roughness of his fingertips sent an additional tremor down her spine as he pushed her bra straps off her shoulders. "I didn't expect you to have calluses," she murmured.

His chuckle rumbled from deep in his chest. "Why? 'Cause I look like a girly-man?"

Her bra dropped away from her breasts and she realized he'd unhooked it when he unzipped her dress. She fought the urge to cover herself. "Hardly. But you don't exactly dig ditches for a living."

He brushed her hair to the side and kissed her neck. "Not in the last ten years, at least. We MacDougals may be privileged, but we sure as hell aren't spoiled." He freed her arms from the straps and nudged the gown down over her hips. It dropped soundlessly to the floor at her feet. "I occasionally go rock climbing with my oldest brother, Wilder. But not so much since he got married."

"Rock climbing. Hmm." She yielded to her modesty and crossed her arms to cover her bare breasts, too aware of the inequity in their state of dress. "Is that why your fingers are so nimble, too?"

"I think I'll plead the Fifth on that one."

Rose's stomach tightened with a fierce jealousy she didn't want to feel. To keep him from suspecting she cared in the slightest, she quipped, "That many women, eh?"

"That many years of piano lessons." He slipped his blunt fingers into the waistband of her panty hose. She prayed it was too dark for him to get a good look at them. She kept talking, in part to draw his attention away from her less-than-sexy hosiery, in part to distract herself from how close she was to coming unglued by the moist warmth of his breath on her neck, his rough fingers on her oversensitive skin.

"Why wouldn't you want to admit to that? I wouldn't have been the least bit surprised to find out a charmer like you can play the piano."

"That's just it." He started to push her nylons slowly down over her hips, squatting so he could trail kisses down her spine.

Rose dropped her head forward. It was all she could do not to melt to the floor along with her clothes. For balance she placed a hand on his shoulder.

Against her lower back he breathed, "I can't

play.'' He slipped the panty hose over her knees and kissed the small of her back. "No sense of rhythm. Musically speaking, that is. Didn't you wonder why we never made it to the dance floor tonight?''

Her throat tight with anticipation of where his mouth might wander next, she half moaned, "Uh-huh.''

He took off a high-heeled shoe, dropping it with a clunk on the hardwood floor, and freed one foot from her panty hose. "Well, despite how much I wanted to hold you in my arms—still do, by the way—'' he kissed wetly where her upper thigh met the curve of her bottom ''—I didn't want to injure your feet by stepping on them.''

Fearing she'd faint from the sexual tension building inside her, she gripped his tux jacket in her fist and carefully lifted her foot so he could take off her remaining shoe and peel the panty hose from her. "I'm sure we could have managed.'' Though they probably never would have made it out of her car, panty hose or no, if he'd held her in his arms on the dance floor.

He tossed the nylons aside. "Let's just say Harry Connick Jr. has nothing to fear from me. But I did end up with nimble fingers.'' He proved it by running them up the outsides of her legs as he straightened behind her.

When his fingers reached her hips, he turned her to face the free-standing oval mirror. Nothing more than a looming shadow behind her fairness, he traced a path to her moist heat with one hand, and reached across her to cup her breast with his other.

Rose went limp against him as his fingers worked their magic on her, stroking, delving, calluses rasping against sensitive skin. The sensations were more than she could bear.

Turning in his arms, she grabbed hold of the lapels of his tuxedo jacket. "You are way overdressed."

He kissed her deeply, and reached back to unfasten his cummerbund. She didn't waste any time, pulling his jacket off his shoulders and down his arms as far as she could, then starting on the onyx studs down the front of his shirt. Brendan somehow managed to unfasten his cuff links without seeing what he was doing, sending them clinking onto the hardwood floor, and pulled open his pants with enough enthusiasm to pop the hook closure right off.

His urgency sent a fresh jolt of need straight to her core and brought an unexpected fullness to her heart. She dismissed it as ego. What woman wouldn't feel incredible about Brendan MacDougal ripping his clothes off for her? In a fraction of the time he had taken to undress her, Brendan's clothes were on the floor, and he gathered her into his arms.

The hair on his chest made her breasts ache when she brushed against him, so she wrapped her arms around his neck tightly and flattened herself to him.

Without her high heels, she fit perfectly beneath the shelter of his strong jaw, and his heat felt so right pressing into her.

A faint voice inside her head begged her to never let go, but she firmly reminded herself that tonight was about the moment, the here and now. They would satisfy each other's physical needs and that would be the end of it.

Her emotional needs would stay locked up in the dark where they belonged. Safe from Brendan L. MacDougal.

Chapter Nine

The feel of Rose's soft, smooth body pressed against his nearly sent Brendan's libido through the roof, but there was something about the way she held on to him that kept him grounded. His instincts had been right. This was a woman who hadn't been given what she wanted, what she deserved, in a very long time. If ever.

A pressure grew in his chest that had nothing to do with the grip she had on him. It was time to lighten things up.

He grinned against her silky hair. "I'm thinking you're in need of a little homage." He was nothing if not a "can-do" kind of guy.

She leaned away from him and met his gaze. "Homage?"

The skeptical quirk of her full lips was irresistible. He brought his head down and caught her lower lip between his, then murmured, "Yeah. Homage."

With a swift movement, he scooped her up into his arms.

The heat of her skin had deepened the scent of her light, sweet perfume, and it filled his head until he could think of nothing besides covering her body with his own. He laid her on her bed's dark comforter, the color indistinct in the dim light, and noticed while he fished among his clothes for the condoms that the bed was an old-fashioned four-poster.

"Nice bed. Antique?"

She bent one knee and draped it over the other, then stretched her hands above her head in such a sexy way his hair should have caught on fire. "Mm-hmm. So is most of my other stuff. I love antiques because they have so much history."

"History is good."

She made a sound low in her throat and turned her face into one of the two pillows at the head of the bed. He was glad to see she hadn't decorated with mounds of frou-frou pillows the way a lot of women did.

The only thing that would get in his way tonight was the long body pillow at the foot of the bed. He quickly donned protection and shoved the huge pillow to the floor with his foot as he settled himself down next to her gorgeous, lithe body. Tonight she'd be wrapping herself around nothing but him.

At that thought alone he nearly rolled on top of

her to get right to the main event—especially when she tugged on his shoulders, encouraging him to— but he forced himself to focus on taking her to a place he'd bet the MacDougal fortune she didn't get to often enough, if ever.

She was so beautiful, so passionate, and he was a man who never backed down from a challenge. So he ignored her soft hands on his shoulders, in his hair, and started his exploration of Dr. Rose Doeber.

He settled his hand just below one full breast, his thumb and fingers framing it, and gave her his best lazy grin. ''Now, I already know what your neck tastes like, but I've ordered chocolate fudge swirl ice cream all my life for a reason. When I find something I like—'' he licked the pulse point high on her elegant neck ''—I go back to it again—'' lick ''—and again.''

He kissed and licked his way down her throat until he reached the top of her chest, where he paused. ''But I also think it's good to try new things. Explore new territory.'' He kissed one breast while his hand traveled up to the other.

By the time he reached her pebbled nipples with his mouth and hand, she was squirming and moaning low in her throat. It was all he could do not to cover her with his body and bury himself deep inside her. He'd never wanted a woman so much in his life. But he was a man of his word.

She raised her head and rasped, ''What?''

He realized he'd said the last part out loud. "Nothing. But damn, you're incredible. You are just so…right." He proved his point by filling his hand with her breast and dropping his knee between her legs. A perfect fit. She responded by rolling toward him to press her body more completely against his. Her soft, short curls rubbed against his arousal, and it was his turn to groan.

He gripped her hip and pushed her onto her back again. "Not yet. Too much uncharted territory."

She buried her hands in his hair and pulled his mouth close to hers. "You can do that later. For round two."

"You're assuming I'll survive round one. It's killing me just touching you. Imagine what being inside you, grinding against you, will do to me."

"Brendan," she begged.

He took pity on her long enough to kiss her hard and deep. His hand strayed downward of its own volition. The slick heat he found set his blood on fire, and he discovered a man had his limits.

Besides, round two would work.

When he shifted on top of Rose and settled himself against her, he decided he liked the idea of round three and four, too. She wrapped her arms and legs around him and he knew if any woman could get him there, she was the one.

He pushed into her, and almost turned inside out right then and there. Nothing had ever felt as good as being wrapped in the fierceness of Rose. It was more than he'd expected. More than he'd wanted. And he didn't have the will to resist.

She urged him deeper. The more he touched her, shared with her, the more something within him connected with her. And the less likely it became that he'd be able to chalk this up to being nothing more than a good time.

They moved together in union, in opposition, and not at all. Everything was beyond his experience. Worth the risk.

Just as he began to doubt his endurance and strength of will, she arched against him and called out, and the last of Brendan's resistance crumbled. He ended up going to a place he knew he'd never been. Judging by the way she clung to him, she'd never been there, either.

He rolled to his side, taking her with him. No matter how much his failure to remain emotionally detached from Rose worried him, he wasn't willing to sever their connection yet. Everything could still be okay. He just needed to get used to what she did to him. Odds were that round two wouldn't rock his universe quite this much.

To prove the theory, he kissed her jaw and neck again until he hardened within her.

Rose drew in a breath that rubbed her breasts against his chest. "Holy cow. You ready to go again already?"

"It seems that not only did I survive, but I'm still hungry for you."

"Wow. Okay." She gave a deep, throaty laugh of amazement that he caught beneath his lips when he kissed her.

She pulled away. "Wait. First tell me your middle name."

He blinked. "What?"

"Tell me your middle name."

"What does that have to do with round two?"

"I need to know what the *L* stands for."

He raised his eyebrows. "Now?"

"Yes. Right now."

With the suspicion he was forever doomed to be confused by the mysteries of women, he answered, "Logan."

"Logan," she repeated, a wistful look on her face that made him need to kiss her.

So he did, good and long.

Out of necessity he separated from her to exchange old protection for new. She crawled beneath the covers, but when he slipped between the sheets he encouraged her to return to the position she'd claimed in the car.

And damn if she didn't blow his mind again.

Though this time his recovery took a little longer.

After a trip to the shower, where he completed his exploration of the sumptuous Dr. Doeber, Brendan had no choice but to accept that the heights he'd reached with Rose the first time had been no fluke. That the woman made him feel as he'd never felt before.

It scared him.

Enough that he was still awake long after she'd cried uncle and drifted off to sleep in his arms. It wasn't the first time he'd lain awake while a beautiful woman used his shoulder as her pillow. But this was the first time his mind hadn't already moved on to the next day's appointments, and what type of bouquet he'd send to her, since he might not actually see her again for a long time after they parted in the morning.

All Brendan could think of tonight was how to keep Rose from shutting him out again the instant the sun came up. Though she hadn't actually let him in any way other than physically. Or had she?

She'd told him what she wanted most in the world—to adopt Dylan—and Brendan was smart enough to see the depth of hunger in her eyes when he moved inside of her. She was not a woman who played games, but rather one who didn't want a traditional relationship any more than he did.

The reminder reassured him. The steady rhythm of her heart, beating in counterpoint to his, lulled him to the edge of sleep. Then Rose flinched and her entire body tensed. He instinctively clutched her to him. She keened softly deep in her throat, clearly in the grip of a nightmare.

Brendan's physical response to her despair was immediate and wholly visceral. It tore at his gut to know she was frightened, even if it might be by something imaginary.

He held her close and soothed her by gently rubbing her back and murmuring, "It's all right, sweetheart. You're okay. You're not alone. I'm here, Rose. I'm here with you. Nothing can hurt you while I'm here."

She grew still and seemed to fall back into a more peaceful sleep, though there was no denying her grip on his chest was tighter than it had been before.

And Brendan surprised the hell out of himself by feeling glad.

ROSE WOKE UP with the heart-pounding start that normally hit her after she'd dozed off over her paperwork during a thirty-six hour rotation. Only it wasn't a copy of a patient's chart stuck to her cheek. It was Brendan Logan MacDougal's chest hair. His breathing was deep and steady, moving her head gently up and down, encouraging her racing pulse to slow and her body to relax again.

Judging by the weak light filtering into the room through the closed miniblinds, it was still early in the morning. But morning, nonetheless. She hadn't planned on having Brendan stay the whole night. Any more than she'd planned to have her world turned on end by his touch.

Both had happened.

She'd fallen asleep in his arms—something she'd decided she was incapable of doing with a man. With anyone. Not even when she cuddled with Dylan in his bed, the weight of exhaustion crushing her. Rose was unwilling to take the chance of having one of the nightmares that had haunted her since she was a child waking up in the hospital without a past. Then Dylan would wake up scared, too.

But she'd fallen asleep with Brendan, and hadn't jerked awake to escape the formless terror she'd never been able to conquer, no matter how much she knew about the workings of the brain. What was it about this man that made him capable of firing every synapse she had, then lull her into a peaceful sleep in his arms?

Could she find that peace again? Did she dare allow herself to? She closed her eyes and breathed in the smell of him, disturbingly familiar because he'd used her soap in the shower during the night. Or rather *she'd* used her soap on him. The memory made her squirm against him.

His hand moved on her back. "Good morning." His deep voice was not quite as silky as usual, which made it even sexier in a way. She couldn't win.

She lifted her head and met his sleepy gaze. The memory of what they'd done in the night—his enjoyment of it—was plain in his hazel eyes.

She blushed. "Good morning." Her own voice sounded raw and unguarded.

His gentle smile made it okay. "Sleep well?"

Brushing back the strands of her hair that clung to the reddish-brown stubble on his jaw, she moved a little away from him. And instantly missed his heat. The arm he'd kept loosely around her tightened. "Apparently." She waited for him to contradict her, but he didn't. Had she really gone a night without nightmares? "Though not all that long, thanks to you."

His grin widened. "Hey, I stopped the second you wanted me to."

"It wasn't so much that I *wanted* you to stop, but one of us had to be sensible. Besides, I need to get to the hospital pretty early, so I can be there when Dylan wakes up."

Brendan reached up and tucked her hair behind her ear. "He's an awfully lucky kid to have you, Rose. You're not only beautiful and brilliant, but reliable, too."

His praise raised more heat in her cheeks on its way to lodging firmly in her heart. Not knowing how to respond to the sensation, she brushed it off. "What I am is late. Dylan is an early riser."

"How much longer does he has to stay in the hospital?"

"Until they name me his guardian. Or at the very least, his foster parent." The truth had popped out, but it felt right to share it with Brendan like this. Right and good. Talk about a new sensation.

He pulled back his chin. "So he's not there for a physical reason?"

"Technically, no. His digestive problems seem to be well in hand, and the tests I'm running to see why he doesn't speak could be done on an outpatient basis. But I don't want him to have to go through another change."

Brendan traced a path up her neck to tuck her hair back again. "You're walking a fine line, Rose."

She closed her eyes, focusing on how good it felt to be touched instead of the ever-present fear the truth of his words stirred to life. "I know. But as soon as Dylan's father signs the papers, they can start the process."

"Where will Dylan go while you're at work?"

Rose nuzzled her cheek against Brendan's hand. "To the hospital with me. We have an awesome day care for the staff's children. He'll have a ball there."

"Sounds like you have it all worked out."

She opened her eyes at his husky, almost wistful tone, but his expression held only admiration. "I'm trying, Brendan. I'm really trying."

He planted a quick, firm kiss on her lips, then rolled away from her and swung his legs off the bed. His broad, naked back looked as smooth and well-defined as it felt. "We'd better get moving then. I'll call for my ride while you shower."

"No," she said without thinking.

It was her turn not to be ready to say goodbye just yet. And it had nothing to do with how incredibly sexy he looked with his thick, mahogany-colored hair tousled, or the way her breasts ached with the urge to press against his muscular back. "I mean, you don't have to call your driver. It's still early enough that I can drop you off at your hotel."

He gave her a definitely intrigued look over his shoulder. "I'm not staying at a hotel. I leased an apartment."

Last night such news would have sent her running. A leased apartment did not equal a short stay in Chicago. But this morning she wasn't entirely surprised that the revelation filled her chest with warmth and made her smile. Considering what had occurred between them, how safe he made her feel. "Okay, I'll drop you off there on my way to the hospital."

It seemed that not only was she not ready to say goodbye to Brendan yet, she suddenly didn't want last night to be the one-time deal they'd agreed upon. Even the whole weekend wouldn't be enough. She loved the way he made her feel, how she could let go of her worries when she was in his arms.

She reined herself in.

So she felt comfortable with Brendan. It had to be because a leased apartment still wasn't a permanent address. He was going back to New York. She just couldn't let herself forget that was a good thing.

ROSE KNEW MORE THAN A FEW raised eyebrows trailed in her wake as she whistled her way down the hall after leaving the staff day care. She'd received permission from Dylan's caseworker to take him there to play instead of to the pediatric ward's play area. This way he'd get used to the people who ran the day care, as well as the other children he'd encounter on a regular basis.

She had planned to stay and play with him for a while, but when it became clear that Dylan felt right at home, the director sent her on her way. Rose agreed that getting Dylan used to her coming and going while he played would be beneficial to him.

She had to admit the ease with which her sweet little boy was adapting lately wasn't the only reason she felt great. Her whole body still tingled from the parting kiss Brendan had given her when she'd dropped him off at his upscale apartment building, and her step was light from his request to see her again later today. She'd been about to ask the same of him, but the fact that he'd asked first made the moment that much better.

As Rose approached the nurses' station Delores did a double take, not trying to hide her surprise at finding Rose the source of the cheery whistling. "Win the lottery or something?"

Rose propped her elbows on the high counter and smiled. "Something like that."

Delores considered her a moment, then heaved a sigh. "I can't believe I'm about to do this." She reached for a stack of pink message slips, muttering as she thumbed through them. "Can't remember the last time I saw such a twinkle in those big blue eyes of yours. If ever."

The nurse paused at one slip, sighed again, then pulled it from the stack and handed it to Rose. "But I know you need to see this."

A sense of foreboding brought Rose firmly back to earth. She took the slip and read it.

"Bobby Ray Evans called. Saw the picture of Dylan with Rory MacDougal. Wants to know what's up with *his son's* new modeling career."

Rose's blood froze. What she'd feared all along had happened. Bobby Ray had seen the picture. And he was claiming Dylan as his son.

She started to shake, then her blood turned to liquid fire as she realized how her worst nightmare had become reality.

Brendan MacDougal had betrayed her.

Chapter Ten

"How *dare* you? How dare you renege on our deal?"

Brendan pulled in his chin, his intense pleasure at discovering Rose knocking on his penthouse door evaporating in the face of her anger. Her color was high, her eyes glittering. Her hair had partially escaped the twist she had clipped it up in this morning.

Concerned and more than a little confused, he frowned. "What are you talking about?"

"Don't play cute and dense with me."

That sent his eyebrows upward.

She leveled a finger at him. "You know exactly what I'm talking about. And because of you, I might lose—" Her voice cracked. What he could now see undeniably as tears glistening in her big blue eyes broke free and ran down her flushed cheeks.

A wrenching compulsion hit him, similar to the one that had sent him to her side the first time he'd seen her. Only much, much stronger. He reached for her.

She dodged his hands and slipped past him into the penthouse. She looked around and let loose a bitter laugh. "Oh, yeah. Nice *apartment.* I should have known you'd be in a penthouse. Very appropriate for a man used to getting whatever he wants."

Brendan raised his brows again as he closed the door. She headed for the bright, spacious living room, using the sleeve of her dark blue sweater to wipe away her tears. He followed her. She muttered darkly as she took in the huge, curving sectional, a great place to watch the sun set over the city beyond the floor-to-ceiling windows. Something he'd planned on doing with Rose this very evening. The realization that he might not get the chance put a vise grip on his chest.

Whatever had happened was far worse than when Rose had discovered Dylan in Rory's race car.

Brendan approached her slowly. "Rose. Honey. Please, what's this about? What happened?"

"Dylan's father, that's what!"

Brendan's gut tightened.

How dare you renege on our deal?

There had been only one bargain struck between them. "Did he contact you about seeing Dylan's picture?"

She whirled to face him. "Of course he contacted me! Exactly what I said would happen happened.

He left a message telling me he saw the photo of 'his son'—'' she waved the pink piece of paper at him ''—and wants to know what's up with Dylan's new modeling career. He thinks that baby, who he's probably never even seen, is worth something now.''

She pushed a wayward lock of hair from her face with a shaky hand. ''He'll never relinquish his parental rights. I'll never be able to give Dylan the security he needs. That he deserves!''

Pivoting away from him, she headed toward the windows. ''I should have known. I should have known better.'' She spread her arms wide, her anger seeming to be aimed more at herself than him. ''I mean, it's not like I haven't been used before. People will always get what they want, no matter what, no matter who gets hurt.''

Brendan couldn't stand to see her so upset. His insides twisted with something far beyond empathy, with no small amount of the feeling stemming from the knowledge that someone had used her. ''Rose, I didn't break our agreement. The fund-raising campaign stayed local.''

''How can you say that when I've proof to the contrary right here?'' She raised a fist, the pink message slip crushed in her grip. ''How can you say that after what we—after how I let you...so close?''

His heart contracted. Obviously she was talking about more than just their physical intimacy. She'd shared her plans with him, her dreams for the future. "I didn't betray your trust, Rose. The campaign stayed local," he repeated.

She let loose an unmistakable sound of disgust. "Yeah, like I can trace my roots back to the *Mayflower*." She waved her hand. "You know what? I just need to go. Don't ask me why I came in the first place. As if you'd admit to going back on your word." She headed for the door.

He moved to stop her. "Rose—"

She held up her hand as she passed him. "Don't make it worse than it already is, Brendan. I mean it. Oh…" She paused, digging in the front pocket of her jeans. She pulled out a white cloth handkerchief. "Here. This is yours." She stepped just close enough to hand it to him, but he was able to snag the pink message slip along with the handkerchief without her notice.

"Now we're done." Shaking her head, she continued to the door. "I can't believe I actually started to think…well, this is what I get, I guess."

He clenched his jaw, frustration welling almost out of control. Rose was condemning him the same way the donors here in Chicago had. "So you've tried and judged me. Just like that?"

She swiped another tear away before reaching for the doorknob. "I'm afraid I'm working off experience, here."

So she'd been hurt before. A spurt of anger on

her behalf, mixed with a splash of wholly selfish jealousy that she'd cared for someone else who'd hurt her, made a fitting chaser to his frustration. Man, had he lost control.

Eyeing the door handle, she said, ''You broke your word. The story got to Bobby Ray. And Dylan and I will pay the price. Goodbye, Brendan.''

He couldn't think of a way to stop her other than physically restraining her. She opened the door and left without looking back.

Brendan stood there, stunned by how easily she'd thought the worst of him. Once again, his credibility had ended up in the toilet. He should be angry. Damn angry, because this time he wasn't to blame. He'd upheld his end of the bargain, so much so he was worried that the lack of exposure would affect the success of the campaign.

But the pressure growing in his chest, crowding his lungs, wasn't indignation. It was more a feeling of loss. Not only didn't he want to be kicked out of Rose's life for supposedly reneging on his word, he didn't want to be kicked out of her life at all.

At least not yet.

But first things first. Despite Brendan's insistence that the picture of Dylan be used only in Chicago, Bobby Ray had somehow managed to find out about it. The logical first step would be to discover how. The easiest and probably most productive way would be to go see the source of Rose's troubles in person.

With the right sort of encouragement, Bobby Ray might see his way clear to give Brendan the proof he'd need to regain Rose's respect. Which was just one of the things he wanted back from her. The way she'd looked at him when she'd trusted him, the way she'd smiled despite herself, her reverent touch. All the things that made him feel like a man, not simply another MacDougal.

Most importantly, he wanted to reassure her that she hadn't been used again. Then he'd find out who'd hurt her the first time, and if at all possible, make him pay.

ROSE HAD NEVER CONSIDERED herself a coward. But the sight of Brendan in his suede jacket and blue jeans leaning against the nurses' station counter, getting Delores to actually giggle, made her seriously consider turning on her heel and running in the opposite direction. He wasn't wearing a tuxedo, or flexing his bare back, or doing any of the other things that had made her believe fantasies could come true. He made her question her emotional strength by doing nothing more than standing with his weight supported on his forearms, his thick, mahogany-brown hair bearing the marks of his fingers.

She didn't think she'd made any noise that would give her presence away, yet Brendan jerked his head in her direction and effectively nailed her to the spot with the determination that settled on his gorgeous face.

Her heart started pounding, energizing her muscles, pumping blood to heat her skin. Not because of any flight instinct. It was as if the last two days of misery had never happened, as if she hadn't convinced herself the ache in her chest and her inability to sleep stemmed from her fear of failing Dylan.

As if she didn't miss a man who wasn't hers to miss.

With a parting comment that made Delores give him a thumbs-up, Brendan pushed off from the high counter and strode toward Rose like an astronaut about to make history. A man born with the right stuff.

But if he thought he had the skill to control whatever explosion he expected from her, he was sadly mistaken. Nothing had changed.

She crossed her arms firmly over her chest and tapped the chart she held against her ribs.

He met her air of annoyance with an altogether too sexy grin. "Dr. Doeber. Just the woman I came to see."

She'd thought she'd sufficiently steeled herself against him, but her body still reacted to the silky depth of his voice. She shifted her weight to stiffen at least one knee. "Why is that? Considering we have nothing to say to each other."

"Oh, I have plenty to say to you, but first…" He reached into the breast pocket of his suede jacket. The same pocket where he'd kept his handkerchief in his tuxedo.

The memory of that act of tenderness made her eyes burn. Why couldn't he have been the man she'd first thought he was, a fantasy man who would never hurt her?

He withdrew some folded papers. "I want to give you this." He unfolded them and offered them to her.

She didn't look at them. "I don't want anything from you." Not even the shelter of his strong arms or being compared to a princess. If she kept saying it, it would be true. It had to be. She didn't have it in her to care about him, only to have him abandon her.

He raised a cocky eyebrow. "You don't want the papers Bobby Ray signed allowing Dylan to be adopted?"

Rose's breath caught in her throat and her arms dropped away from her chest, the chart in her hand forgotten. She jerked her gaze to the papers he held. They were indeed the necessary documents. She'd seen them before, and knew exactly where Bobby Ray's signature needed to be on the last one.

Her chest pulsed with joy, but her brain rejected the notion, just as it had rejected the possibility of Brendan being her perfect man when he'd first stepped into her life. He'd managed to give her the comfort she'd needed that night, but she'd been disappointed far too many times in her life to believe he could give her this, her heart's desire.

"Take them, Rose. They're for real."

She reached for the papers, not at all surprised her hand was shaking, and flipped to where Bobby Ray's signature should be. It was there, a scratchy, arrogant scrawl. He'd given up his parental rights, freeing Dylan for adoption. The gate that had been closed to her, keeping her from what she wanted more than anything, had been thrown open.

By a dream man come to life.

She shook her head and firmly reminded herself that Brendan had just recently complicated matters with Bobby Ray.

"Oh, and this, too." He went fishing inside his jacket again and pulled out a white envelope someone had ripped.

"What's that?"

"Proof."

"Proof of what?"

"That I kept my word. That I didn't renege on our deal."

Not sure if she could take having him truly be her dream man, Rose hesitated.

Brendan gave her a slightly exasperated look and held the envelope so she could see the address. "This was sent to one Bobby Ray Evans, currently a resident of Folsom Prison, from one—" he turned the envelope so he could read the front of it "—James Nelson.

"Mr. Nelson resides not all that far from here, is

apparently a long time, er, business associate of Mr. Evans, and is currently limited to his home and work by court order and a nifty ankle bracelet. Thanks to electronic monitoring and his surprising lack of a television, Mr. Nelson has been forced to occupy himself by reading all sorts of newspapers. *Local* newspapers.'' From the envelope Brendan took a newspaper clipping with a note stuck to it. He held it out to her.

The note partially covered the picture of Dylan and Rory in the race car. While the handwriting was nearly illegible, Rose could make out something about a favor being returned.

''I didn't break my word, Rose. Bobby Ray's crony sent him the picture. I agree it was an unfortunate, and potentially disastrous, by-product of my wish to use Dylan's photo—something I truly hadn't believed would happen—but it wasn't a result of not keeping the photo local.''

''How did you—?''

He shrugged with the nonchalance capable only by men like him. Men who never failed to get their way. ''Visiting hours are nine to five.''

''You *visited* Bobby Ray? In California?''

''You're a woman of strong...well, let's just call them convictions, Rose. Something I greatly admire, by the way. I knew you'd only believe me if I provided you with proof.''

He took a step closer, his warmth and size reminding her of their intimacies. The hall seemed to fade away, and she longed to slip into his strong embrace. "I've had enough doubts about the value of my word lately. There was no way I was going to allow you to continue doubting it, also."

Her world spinning, Rose scrabbled for emotional solid ground by trying to focus on the details rather than the implications, the hope. "How did you get Bobby Ray to sign over his parental rights?"

Brendan shrugged again, shifting closer. "Same way I got him to give me the newspaper clipping. I simply mentioned, sort of offhandedly, that I have a lot of friends in the California prison system. On the administration side, of course, not the resident side. Believe it or not, there are worse places to be than where Bobby Ray is in Folsom. Transfers happen all the time...."

Rose gaped. "You threatened him?"

He shook his head. "MacDougals don't threaten. No need to." He reached up and brushed her hair back from her face as if he'd done it a thousand times before. "I simply mentioned a few things. How Bobby Ray interpreted them was entirely up to him. And it's not as if the scumbag didn't deserve a scare, after what he put you through."

Brendan had championed her. Rose's throat contracted and her eyes burned. She knew she should thank him, but she couldn't find the words. She didn't know how to find them. No one had ever championed her before.

With a soft, understanding smile that set fire to the fortress around her heart, he whispered, ''You're welcome.''

Rose lost herself in the warmth of his hazel eyes, her chest hurting as the reality of what he'd given her took hold.

''So, are we friends again?''

With her future blown wide with possibilities, she made an effort to find her voice. ''Is that what you want to be?''

His expression heated unmistakably. ''*Good* friends.''

Her body responded as if he'd touched her, but her mind stayed in charge. ''I think it might be a good idea to slow things down a little, though. We kind of skipped a couple stages.''

''Sure. Whatever you say.'' Even as he agreed he lowered his head, his gaze fastened on her lips. ''I want to learn everything there is to know about Dr. Rose Doeber.''

His words hit her like a sneak attack with defibrillator paddles. And the fact that she was about to let him kiss her in full view of the pediatric floor's nurses' station jolted her more.

But worst of all by far, a huge part of her suddenly didn't care.

BRENDAN HAD INTENDED to clear his name with Rose, do something she deserved to have done for her, then be on his way. But the look on her beautiful face as she'd tried to thank him for getting Bobby Ray's signature on the papers, officially clearing the way for her adoption of Dylan, had rooted him to the spot.

Now he wanted to stay.

He wanted to keep that glow of wonder and bone-deep happiness in her expression as long as possible. The desire had nothing in common with his love of making important things happen for people, for bringing to fruition projects that others believed were hopeless. The main reason he enjoyed his job running the MacDougal Foundation so much.

This was selfish. Making Rose happy made him happy in a way he'd never experienced before.

He wanted the feeling to last.

Her mouth was welcoming when he caught it beneath his own with slow, gentle purpose. He tried to express what he knew he shouldn't say in the kiss. That she was special to him.

Just as Rebecca Crestfield had been special to him.

He ended the kiss abruptly. What was he thinking, taking his relationship with Rose to the next level? He exhaled shakily, fighting for control of not only his body but his common sense. "You know, I really should get back to my place and finish crunching the numbers from the auction.''

She blinked a few times before the glaze generated by their kiss cleared from her eyes. A very different kind of satisfaction surged through him, heaping more proof on the conclusion he'd already drawn. Rose was far more dangerous to him emotionally than Rebecca had been.

Her smile was weak and uneven. ''Oh. Okay.'' She drew herself up, and he knew she was regaining command of herself, too. ''Actually, that's good. I also have work to do. And a speech therapist is coming to see Dylan. She thinks she might be able to at least get him to make sounds.''

It took everything in Brendan to fight the desire to be present when that happened. ''I hope she's successful.'' He forced himself to take a step back. Then another. ''Well, I'd better go.''

She raised a hand slightly in a halfhearted farewell, confusion sneaking into the depths of her blue eyes.

Brendan made himself turn and walk away.

Despite his determination not to allow it, she stirred something deep within him, reached a part of him he'd vowed to never leave vulnerable again.

His heart.

Chapter Eleven

Restless, Brendan paced the length of Dr. Williams's office. Even with the older man's assurances to the contrary before he had been called away, Brendan seriously doubted Rose would be willing to help him out once again with his fund-raising, especially after the incident with the Van Hovens. And he had nothing to bargain with this time.

But he needed her again, even more.

The door opened, and Rose came in.

Two days had passed since they'd last spoken, and his pulse revved at the sight of her. Her beauty never ceased to surprise him. Only now, images of what she looked like, felt like, tasted like in his arms added to the broadside effect. Knowing exactly what lay beneath her white lab coat, tan T-shirt and snug black pants made his mouth dry.

When her bright blue eyes landed on him, she halted a step over the threshold. "Brendan?"

He cleared his throat. "Hello, Rose."

She glanced around. "I thought Dr. Williams—"

"He had something he had to attend to, but he graciously lent me the use of his office so I could speak to you." Brendan moved to close the door behind her.

She had no choice but to come farther into the room. "I'd started to think I'd never hear from you again."

"I've been in New York."

"Ah. Though I've never been there, I could have sworn I heard somewhere that they have phones, too."

A smile tugged at his mouth. Despite his irrational desire to hear the sound of her voice, he'd honored her request to slow things down. But maybe she didn't want it that badly. The thought brought on a huge smile and a telling warmth in his chest. "They do. I know because I've been on the phone the entire time I was gone, trying to salvage this charity campaign."

Her eyes widened. "It needs salvaging? I thought the auction had gone well."

He ran a hand through his hair, frustration returning full force. "Not well enough. Thanks to my tarnished reputation, the foundation didn't raise the capital needed to move forward with the expansion of the pediatric program here. There's more money to be raised."

She crossed her arms and grumbled something

about blind jerks. "And you're telling me this now because…?"

"Because I need your help again. The only really positive buzz about the auction had to do with you. The donors were impressed by you. Simple as that."

Her arms dropped away from her chest.

He dared to move closer to her, focusing on what he needed to convince her of to keep from touching her smooth cheek or running his hand over the silky softness of her hair. "Time is running out for me to honor my obligations to the hospital and meet their desired timeline for expansion, so I can't take any chances. I'm having to pull out the big guns and go out of state, holding a function at MacDougal House attended by any and all available family members. I'd like you to be there, also. You're my pinch hitter, Rose."

She pulled in her chin, clearly skeptical. "Your *pinch hitter?*"

"We make a great team." He gave up fighting the urge to touch her and ran his fingertips along her jaw. "I need you, Rose. Please say you'll help me by coming to this last fund-raiser."

She closed her eyes and brought her delicate blond brows together. "You said something about going out of state?"

Hit by the thought of how much his parents would like Rose, he said, "Yes. New York City. Some very generous people I'm hoping will support this project live there, and have been invited to the dinner and reception I've arranged at MacDougal House. It'll be a quick overnight trip.''

She opened her eyes, her gaze filled with all sorts of doubt. "I can't leave—"

"Yes, you can. I've already discussed this with Dr. Williams. He can take care of Dylan as well as cover for you, like he did before. It's all set."

"I really wish you two wouldn't decide these things without speaking with me first—"

He stopped her with a finger to her smooth lips. And instantly regretted it. All his logical, well-thought-out arguments went out of his head at the feel of that delicate skin and the moist heat of her breath. "Please, Rose. The hospital needs you. All those kids need you to step up to the plate again. I need you."

Then he did what he'd been thinking about since he'd last seen her. He kissed her.

ROSE HAD NO DEFENSE against being needed, just as she had no defense against the heavenly firmness of Brendan's lips. No matter what immunity she might have built up since the last time he'd unwittingly played on her greatest weaknesses, she already knew she would succumb again this time. He had done so much for her.

He was still in her system.

So much so that she'd spent the past two nights

considering the possibility of a future with him. But she kept getting hung up on whether she could have a future with him without revealing the past he seemed determined to know. The way his mouth felt on hers, she decided it was worth a try.

She opened her lips beneath his, and he deepened the kiss with a groan that lifted her against him. She'd hated herself for missing him so much, for missing how his tongue felt against hers. But when he gathered her into his arms and explored her mouth she realized it was little wonder. The man knew how to kiss.

He also knew exactly how to hold her, sheltered but anchored, and how to touch her as if she was both precious and real. And he looked at her as if he saw her, Rose, not Dr. Doberman, or Little Lost Rose, or Little Miss Nobody. How could she not have missed him?

Whether a future with him was in the cards or not, she'd accept what he had to give her for the time being.

Because living with Brendan in the moment was a slice of heaven she wanted more than her next breath.

He pulled his mouth away from hers and let out a shaky sigh against her hair. ''So, you'll come with me to New York?''

She closed her eyes, allowing herself a moment of suspended bliss wrapped in his heat before she took the step that might very well send her off yet another cliff with this man. "Can we leave Chicago late and get back early?"

"One definite perk of having a corporate jet at my disposal is coming and going on my schedule, not someone else's. The reception doesn't start until seven tomorrow night. You'll have most of the day to see patients and be with Dylan."

A corporate jet. More likely a private jet. "Yes, that definitely is *one* perk."

He chuckled, and the deep sound transferred to her chest in the most wonderful way. "Good thing, too, because I have to fly home tonight to finalize some things. But I'll return in plenty of time to get you—here at the hospital, if you prefer."

She spread her fingers over the smoothness of his cream knit shirt. He came in and out of her life so easily, but still managed to leave her defenses in ruins. It wasn't as if he'd laid siege to her. She'd more or less opened the gates to him. "That's fine."

"Good. I'll call and confirm the time tomorrow." He planted a kiss on her hair and stepped back, leaving her feeling a little exposed and vulnerable after their heated embrace. In Dr. Williams's office, no less. Letting her defenses down here was more telling than when she'd kissed him in the pediatrics hallway.

But she'd made the choice to allow him back in

her life. And she already knew the decision was risky.

The question was, how big?

BRENDAN WAS TRUE TO his word. They didn't arrive at MacDougal House in Manhattan until a quarter past six in the sleek black limousine that had picked them up at the Newark airport. After the opulence of the private jet, Rose wasn't surprised by the type of car waiting for them, or its "Mac 2" license plate. But she was utterly speechless to discover that MacDougal House was not some community facility with a prime location and named for its benefactors, or even the MacDougal Foundation's base of operations.

She came to a halt in the grand foyer bustling with activity in preparation for the night, her mouth dropping open when the tall, balding butler said, "Welcome home again, Brendan. And welcome to MacDougal House, Dr. Doeber. I hope your flight was uneventful."

As Brendan assured the butler, named Sean, that it had been, Rose looked around wide-eyed at what seemed like acres of white-and-gray marble floors warmed by richly colored rugs, towering columns of the same marble, tremendous vases filled with fresh flowers and dozens of large painted portraits. She glanced back at Brendan, stunned that this huge, obviously historic mansion was his family home.

Just to make sure, after she acknowledged Sean's welcome with a smiling nod, she leaned toward Brendan and whispered, "You *live* here?"

"When I'm in New York, yep."

She shook her head and looked up at the molded ceiling at least two stories above her, muttering, "*Yep*. The man lives in an honest-to-goodness mansion and he says things like 'yep.'"

Brendan laughed and took her arm, snuggling her against him. "Come on. We don't have much time to get changed and back down here before the first guests arrive. I also want to have the chance to introduce you to the members of my family who'll be attending tonight in an attempt to save my rear."

Her nervousness increasing with each step, Rose let him lead her to a grand marble staircase that split at a wide landing halfway up. Not only was she going to be in the spotlight again, but she would be meeting Brendan's family. From the way he'd spoken of them on the plane, they seemed to be close-knit—something completely foreign and almost mythical to Rose. Why hadn't she keyed into that part when he'd asked her to come?

Because she hadn't heard much besides his saying he needed her.

But did a man who lived a life like Brendan's in a world like this really need anything, much less a few earnest comments about the needs of less fortunate children from a nobody like her?

Thanks to him, though, she wasn't as much of a nobody as she had been. She was on her way to being Dylan's mom. The best possible thing in the world.

Brendan deserved her best effort tonight. Despite her apprehensions, she'd give it her all.

As they climbed the stairs to the right, Brendan explained, "This place is big enough that everyone has a set of rooms to themselves that are pretty much self-contained apartments, so I'm not *really* living with my parents."

She grinned at him. "Sorry, pal. If you're all under the same roof, using the same front door, you're still living with the folks." She made light of it, but oh, how she envied him. No wonder he always seemed so at ease, so self-assured. He had the unconditional support of his family.

They stopped at a set of double doors on the right, and Brendan opened them to reveal what did indeed look like the living room of an apartment—an apartment considerably larger than Rose's house—though the kitchen looked more like a wet bar than someplace she'd want to try to cook, limited cooking skills and all.

He went past her and opened a door on the left. "This is your room. I thought you might prefer your own bathroom to get ready in."

She moved toward him and peered inside. The large room was a sea of gender-neutral taupes, creams and browns. Her dress bag hung from the closet door, and the black Gore-Tex backpack she'd brought in lieu of the overnight bag she didn't own sat on a tufted beige bench at the end of a beautiful iron four-poster bed overflowing with sumptuous taupe suede bedding.

Brendan pointed to the door opposite hers across the small foyer. "I'm right over there. Should you need me." He waggled his eyebrows.

Rose blushed, even though there was no one else to see them. "So, any guest of yours stays in your suite? Including business associates?" Which was what she was supposed to be.

"No. There's a regular guest wing, with several suites."

She raised her brows. "And I'm in here because…?"

He leaned against the doorjamb. "Because the guest wing is clear on the other side of the house."

A feeling akin to horror widened her eyes. "What exactly did you tell your family about our…our… relationship?" She mentally winced at the word, remembering the conversation they'd had before he'd come home with her after the auction. Neither of them wanted a relationship. Yet here they were. Was she reading more into this than she should? It was all she could do not to wring her hands.

"I told them you're a very special person I

wanted them to meet. A person who wants to help kids even more than I do. Who, with your passion and caring, has the ability to repair the damage I did to this fund-raising campaign with nothing more than her passionate caring.''

Indignation for him flared hot inside her. ''It wasn't you who did the damage, it was that lying, two-faced crook—''

His smile stopped her tirade. ''They're happy to have you here, Rose. And I wanted you close.''

Her anger dissolved, along with the strength in her knees. Still, she forced herself to consider their accommodation arrangements with a critical eye— for Brendan's sake. ''But won't they worry that you might be...that is, that you may have made the same...'' She trailed off, not wanting to sound like the Van Hovens.

''Mistake?'' He shook his head. ''You're nothing like her, Rose. Nothing at all.''

Unwilling to entirely trust her interpretation of the warmth in his eyes, she joked, ''Because I'm *Dr. Doberman?*''

He ran a finger along her tight jaw. ''Because you're you, Rose. A woman strong enough to champion an idiot like me.''

His words melted her further. But was she strong enough to protect her heart from a man like him if it turned out they had no future together?

She had to be strong enough. That would be one abandonment she doubted she'd survive.

ROSE SLOWLY DESCENDED the grand staircase, wishing she hadn't sent Brendan down earlier, when he'd finished dressing. She'd been nervous enough trying to smooth her hair into a twist without him asking through the bathroom door every five minutes if she needed help. She would have been much more comfortable joining the crowd gathering in the foyer with Brendan's strong arm to hold on to.

Afraid to look up from the stairs for fear of taking a misstep or catching a pointed toe of her shoes on the hem of her gown, she felt several pairs of eyes upon her. What in heaven's name had possessed her to bring only the blue gown for tonight?

Somehow, the idea of doing something to please Brendan in acknowledgment of everything he'd done for her had seemed reasonable when she'd been packing this morning. She wasn't so sure now, after risking a glance at the crowd as she neared the bottom of the steps. It seemed as if all eyes in the place were trained on her. Exactly the reason she hadn't wanted this dress in the first place. Why had she made such a stupid choice?

Her gaze caught on Brendan's and the answer hit her low in the stomach. She'd decided to wear the blue dress because a foolish part of her had hoped to see that hot look of need in his hazel eyes again.

He stepped away from a cluster of downright beautiful, elegantly dressed people and came forward to offer her his hand as she reached the bottom stair. The possessive way he gripped her fingers sent a thrill through her.

He looked her over from head to foot, his eyes positively glowing, heating every inch of her skin. "You wore the blue dress."

The wonder and appreciation in his tone added to the pleasure spreading through her. "I thought you might like it. Though I have to admit, I wouldn't have worn this dress if I'd known MacDougal House was actually your family's home and most of said family would be in attendance."

"Why?"

She shrugged self-consciously. "It's a little much." She rolled a bare shoulder. "Or actually, not enough."

"Nonsense. You're beautiful in it." He leaned close. "You're beautiful *out* of it, too."

Goose bumps erupted across her skin and Rose glanced around to make sure no one was standing close enough to hear. "Brendan!" she scolded. She had no idea who among those mingling in the foyer were family members or newly arrived guests. But when her gaze landed on the group Brendan had been talking with a moment ago she figured she could make a good guess.

The tall, broad-shouldered older gentleman in a

tuxedo, with an unusual red-green-and-purple-plaid vest and bow tie, bore an unmistakable resemblance to Brendan save for his thick gray hair and his overtly curious green eyes. The eyes of the two young women flanking him were also green. Brendan's sisters?

Their resemblance to him was less marked, though the taller of the two—who was far curvier than Rose and looked stunning in a simply cut, beaded cream gown—had the same lustrous, mahogany-colored hair as Brendan. It hung down her back in waves. The other sister, equally elegant though more daring in a black slip dress, had much redder hair, which she wore in a sleek bun. She had the feminine version of Brendan's square shoulders.

A stunning older woman stepped away from Sean the butler and joined the group, her gaze also on Rose. She had to be Brendan's mother, with her dark auburn, chin-length hair tucked behind her ears. She was clearly responsible for the richer tones in his hair. The curiosity in her deep brown eyes was less obvious, though a little harder edged.

Rose couldn't blame her, since the last woman Brendan had partnered with to raise money had betrayed him.

She glanced at him and found him watching her, too, though his gaze was decidedly naughty, his mind obviously still on how she looked naked. Her body joined in the fun, sending a hot flush spreading upward from her chest. She forced herself to think about how she could learn as much as possible about these people without revealing too much about herself. She would hate to see the look on Brendan's face if he were to discover the truth about her now, that she was so different from what he thought her to be.

Perhaps that scam artist had made him wary in more than just his business relationships. For his sake she dearly hoped not. The aching scar from being used by people she'd given her heart to, people who were supposed to be her family forever, wasn't something she'd wish on anyone. Especially not Brendan, such a generous man by nature.

He grasped her hand firmly and she noticed how clammy hers was in contrast. With a wink he guided her toward his family.

His family. Judging by the huge coat of arms hanging over the door behind them and the generations of portraits on the walls, his was a family steeped in history and tradition. The sort of family that provided a kind of security she couldn't imagine.

One very important thing they didn't have in common.

The one thing Rose envied the most.

The one thing she feared she'd never have.

Chapter Twelve

For the first time in his career, Brendan couldn't concentrate on his purpose. Considering how important the success of tonight's function was to him, that said a lot. His mind—not to mention his gaze—kept drifting to the beauty in blue being introduced around the room by his oldest sister, Aileen. They'd collectively decided before Rose came downstairs that it would be better if he and Rose separately worked the gallery full of philanthropists, hand-picked for their history of generosity with out-of-state projects.

The consensus had been, for tonight at least, the less Brendan and Rose appeared to be a couple, the less likely the donors would be reminded of his last close involvement with a woman. A woman who had cost the foundation millions. Rose would have a greater chance of inspiring confidence in donors who, while not as condemning as those in Chicago, still wondered about Brendan's judgment.

His family had been curiously quiet about him bringing another beautiful woman on board to help raise funds. Perhaps because he'd stressed the fact that she was a pediatric neurologist at the hospital he was working to expand and so passionate about the children in her care she was adopting one. If they thought he and Rose were passionate about each other, also, they'd kept it to themselves.

He'd figured putting her up in his suite might cause him some grief. But his mother hadn't commented since she'd taken a place at his side in the informal reception line they'd formed, other than to ask if Rose's needs had been seen to.

As if she knew where his thoughts had wandered and that they'd included her, Mary MacDougal leaned toward him and said softly, ''I'm so pleased to see you getting on with your social life, sweetheart.''

Brendan glanced at her. Maternal satisfaction warmed her dark brown eyes before she shifted her gaze to watch Aileen, now accompanied by his father, introducing Rose around the room. So much for not catching any grief. Having only one of her grown children married off apparently annoyed her to no end.

''This is work, Mom.'' Though it hadn't felt at all like work having his mind blown in bed by a certain beautiful blonde.

His mother made a subtle noise that let him know

she considered him full of it. "Really? I'd assumed that since she's staying in your rooms you two must be involved."

"She's in my guest room. I thought she'd be more at ease there."

"Hmm." His mother didn't sound convinced.

Maybe it showed that he was hoping Rose wouldn't actually sleep in his guest room. She was so beautiful, and aside from a few glances his way that were tinged with worry, she looked very poised and at home talking to New York's notables. More than a few of whom were somehow related to him.

The MacDougals always did know how to rally around one of their own. That they'd had to rally around him gave his pride a serious slap-down. But the foundation needed them, so he would deal with it.

"Well, she's a lovely woman. And so accomplished." His mother elbowed him lightly. "I like that, you know. A woman of real substance, not smoke and mirrors like Rebecca Crestfield. You have no idea how relieved I am that you're no longer allowing that awful experience to cast a shadow over your life."

He let the comment slide. Now was not the time to disillusion his mother by telling her how wrong she was. That the shadow loomed large.

When all the confirmed attendees had arrived,

Brendan and his mother left their place by the doors opening onto the foyer and began mingling in turn.

His mother hooked her arm through his. "Let's go rescue Rose from your father and his brothers. Aileen should know better than to let that bunch be one of Rose's first impressions of this family. You know how they love to tell stories about all the various body parts that have been lopped off and reattached."

"Rose is a doctor, Mom. The kind who's poked at brains. They'd have a hard time grossing her out."

His mother inclined her head. "True. And judging by how serious they all look, they're probably talking about the stock market instead. Still reason enough to rescue your young lady."

"She's not my young lady," Brendan clarified as he let her lead him toward the group consisting of Rose, Aileen, his father, and his uncles Duncan and Orin.

His uncles' last-minute inclusion by his mother on the evening's guest list let Brendan know in no uncertain terms how seriously damaged his parents believed his reputation to be. Duncan and Orin MacDougal had stellar images in the investment community, and their backing would carry a lot of weight, even though they were close relatives.

When Brendan and his mother reached the group, he realized Rose was the one doing the talking. "A child with such an injury shouldn't be moved, much less transported to a different facility. If we can raise the necessary funds, we would be able to expand the pediatric wing enough to accommodate the sort of diagnostic equipment needed to treat children like Ian Stuart without putting him at such risk.''

Duncan immediately started fishing in the breast pocket of his black tuxedo jacket. "How much more are you needing, my dear?''

Brendan blinked as his uncle pulled out his checkbook. Rose had him anteing up already? Apparently Brendan wasn't the only MacDougal who couldn't resist her.

Her cheeks pinkened slightly and she glanced at him. The blue of her eyes had deepened with pleasure. "I think Brendan can speak to that. I'm just here to talk about the hospital's needs.''

As he moved to stand between his uncles, Brendan tried to convey to Rose with a look how proud he was of her. "And you must be doing a fine job as usual if Uncle Duncan is ready to cut a check.'' He clapped a hand on Duncan's shoulder. "I'll take whatever you're willing to give, sir.''

Out of the corner of his eye he noticed that the clusters of guests near them were paying rapt attention to what was going on among the MacDougals. It was all he could do not to kiss his uncle—though Rose was undoubtedly the more appealing and deserving recipient. He'd save that for later, along with a few other activities he'd been thinking about.

Orin elbowed Brendan and pointed to Rose, saying in a loud aside, "Unlike that last one, this one is Mrs. MacDougal material if I ever saw it. Don't let her get away."

While he shouldn't have been surprised by Orin's bluntness, Brendan choked, disguising it with a cough. Rose's attention dropped to the champagne flute in her hands, and Brendan could tell by the rising color in her cheeks that she'd heard.

Brendan should dissuade his uncle, as well as the other family members looking at him expectantly, of the notion that he and Rose were anything other than fund-raising partners. But he couldn't quite force the words out. They *weren't* just partners, and Rose was perfect for the job in so many ways. Her caring, dedicated nature, her poise, her humor, her passion...

But she was also a threat to his heart, something he'd sworn not to bring into the mix.

ROSE SPENT THE EVENING at MacDougal House in a state of constant amazement. Not only was she floored by the mounting evidence of just how wealthy and influential the MacDougals were—after Brendan's Uncle Duncan had pledged his financial support, several other guests Rose had yet to meet offered theirs—but she was nearly overwhelmed by his family's obvious devotion and love for each other.

She was finding it harder and harder not to be swept up in it all.

At first Brendan's sisters had been especially wary of her. Understandably so, given that the last woman he'd enlisted to help him raise money had turned out to be the worst type of thief. But they warmed up to her once they were assured she had a vested interest in raising money for the hospital, and had no pat answers about her designs on their brother, just embarrassing stammers and hot cheeks.

She found herself liking them immensely. The thought of having women such as these as friends, as *sisters,* made her throat tight.

Brendan's parents were more subtle in their probing of her character, and only through years of practice was she able to dodge their questions about her family, or lack thereof. They seemed to think she already knew how badly damaged Brendan's reputation was and how desperate he was to repair it. Her heart ached for him, knowing what a blow it must have been to his pride.

She and Brendan were seated far apart at the impossibly long table for the dinner, to better spread the word of the hospital's need. For Brendan's sake Rose gave it her all, putting herself out there as never before. And thanks to the reliable presence of Brendan's sister Aileen, not once did she worry about the cost of drawing too much attention to herself, or how she might be used. It was an invigorating, freeing sensation, and she didn't want it to end.

But when Brendan joined her and what she belatedly realized was one of the last remaining guests, Rose had no choice but to stop talking about the rehabilitation they could provide children recovering from head trauma. She smiled guiltily and offered to see the guests out. The warmth of Brendan's hand on the small of her back as they walked the last couple to the door was the best sort of compensation. She sent him a grin that hopefully said as much.

The look he gave her held far more meaning, and before she could untangle and decipher the emotions in his hazel eyes, his mother clapped her hands, drawing their attention to where she stood on the stairs. Brendan's sisters and father were already on their way up.

"Well done, everyone. Well done." She bowed her head in appreciation to the white-coated staff already making quick work of the cleanup. "The MacDougal Foundation is in your debt. Dr. Doeber, you in particular did a fine job. Thank you so much for putting faces and names to those who benefit from the money we raise."

Rose shrugged and smiled in acknowledgment,

not sure what she should say, other than, "Please, call me Rose."

Brendan leaned close and whispered, "And the fact that one of the children you talked about happened to have a name as Scottish as Ian Stuart was a nice touch."

She glared at him. "That was not a *nice touch*. It was simply a coincidence."

He laughed and wrapped his arm around her waist to pull her close. "All right, I believe you. You haven't been at this fund-raising stuff long enough to work it that well."

The odd tone in his voice sent a wave of concern through her. "Do you feel like you have to *work it?*"

"Lately, yeah. Not that it does any good."

"Oh, Brendan, you—"

He stopped her with a squeeze. "Later." Releasing her, he stepped away. "Mother, why don't you join Dad." He gestured at his father, already near the top of the stairs, plainly on his way to bed. "This was my shindig, so I'll see to the cleanup."

"Why, thank you, dear. I'll do just that. Rose, if I don't bump into you tomorrow, it was a pleasure to meet you, and hopefully we'll be seeing you again soon." Mary MacDougal waved, then gathered her skirts and climbed the stairs.

Brendan turned back to Rose. "I also have a few

administrative things to see to, so why don't you head up, too?''

''Then we'll talk?''

He gave her a soft, intimate smile. ''Yeah. Then we'll talk. Say, now that you know firsthand all about my family, it's time you finally tell me about yours.'' He ran a finger under her chin before turning to Sean, who seemed to be waiting with a question.

Rose put a hand over her stomach, which had started to roll at the mention of her ''family,'' and hurried for the stairs. Maybe she wouldn't wait up for Brendan, after all.

Because when it came to her family, she had nothing to tell. Only secrets to keep.

ROSE JOLTED UPRIGHT, her heart pounding out of control from the formless threat weighing her down until she feared her skull would crack. A bright light appeared in the darkness, and her eyes focused enough to recognize a man's silhouette against the light.

''Rose?'' A man come to help, not hurt.

The rest of the terror retreated at the sound of Brendan's voice, and she realized he was standing in the doorway of her room in his suite. And that she'd had one of her nightmares. She glanced at the glowing red numbers of the bedside clock: 1:05 a.m.

She'd been asleep for an hour and a half, not having waited up for Brendan.

He came into the room, the light from the door guiding him to where she sat in the middle of the large guest bed, gripping the taupe suede comforter in her hands.

With the light behind him, he seemed not much more than shadow as he sat down on the edge of the bed. "You cried out. Are you okay?"

She ran a hand through her tousled hair, her eyes adjusting to the contrast of light and dark. He was bare-chested, wearing only dark, loose pajama bottoms that tied at the waist. He'd gone to bed, too. His own bed. He must have received the subtle signal that her not waiting up for him meant she didn't want to talk. She wouldn't have been opposed to his climbing into bed and holding her, however.

"Yeah. I just had a bad dream." A dream about doubts and the unknown and fairy tales coming to an end.

He swung his legs up onto the bed and scooted closer to her. "Care to tell me about *this* one?"

The mattress dipped beneath his weight and she used it as an excuse to lean against him. "This one?"

He reached up and brushed a lock of hair away from her face, his touch infinitely gentle. "You had a nightmare the night we spent together."

Her breath froze in her lungs. "Why didn't you say something about it?"

He lifted a muscled shoulder. "Didn't think it was any big deal. I knew you'd had a stressful few days, and figured that was what brought it on. That and not having a man in your bed in…I'm guessing awhile?"

"A very long while, yes."

"So what caused this one? Being in a strange place? Having to put yourself out there again?" His deep voice worked its way between her bones and soothed her like nothing had before.

Warmth radiated from his bare skin as his strong shoulder pressed against hers. Rose found herself wanting to share her demons for the first time in her life. That would be such a risk, though, especially considering the assumptions Brendan had made about her, and the amount of time that had passed without her correcting him.

"What scares you so much, Rose?" he coaxed. "Come on, sweetheart. You know you can trust me."

The last barrier inside her crumbled, and she turned so he could gather her to him. He was right. She *could* trust him. The longer she continued to shut him out, the more damage it would do to their relationship in the long run. As he held her to his warmth and strength, Rose's last doubts dissipated into the night. She wanted a relationship with Brendan and she wanted it for the long run. A very long run.

At least she could be sure he wouldn't use her to gain some sort of notoriety. His family had plenty of their own. They might actually shy away from more. Brendan deserved to have a choice.

Seeing how he handled the truth of her past might be a cruel test to spring on him, but a very foolish part of her needed the truth not to matter to him, needed to know he'd still want her in his life.

And if this fairy tale of hers had to end—which it might, now that they'd raised enough money for the hospital and no longer had an altruistic reason to be together—better to have it end now. On her terms.

She turned her face to his shoulder and breathed in the warm, masculine scent of him, doing her darnedest to hold on to the memory in her brain before she spoke. "It's a nightmare I've had since I was little, but it's really nothing more than shapes and impressions."

He stroked her back through her silky pajama top. "Ones that apparently scare the bejeezus out of you."

"Precisely."

"Have you talked to anyone about it?"

"Oh, yes. But it seems my subconscious is a pretty tough nut to crack. Frankly, I'd rather not know what they mean now."

"Why not?"

She breathed deep. What was it about this man that made her want to put her heart under the scalpel? Maybe it was because she'd met him in a weak moment, allowing him a foot in the door. Even so, if because of her past he wasn't going to want her, then she needed to know now, before her heart was lost to him completely. "Because there's a good chance my mind is, for the most part, protecting me."

His hand on her back stilled. "From what, Rose?"

"From what happened to me before they found me unconscious under a rosebush in a city park at the ripe old age of six. When I woke up, at Chicago General no less, I had no memory of who I was or where I'd come from. I still don't." Her voice cracked, but she made herself continue before Brendan had a chance to say anything that might make her want to stop.

"They named me Rose Doe and ran my picture in a bunch of newspapers and on all the television stations in the region. They turned me into quite a celebrity. Unfortunately, not for a good reason. But despite all the publicity about 'Little Lost Rose,' no one who knew me came forward. A lot of people wanted to adopt me, so they gave me to the most adamant couple. Turns out they only wanted me for the notoriety that came along with me."

She spread her fingers over his chest, burrowing her fingertips beneath the smattering of hair. His heart pounded beneath her touch, but she didn't allow herself to consider why, trying to distance herself from her words as much as she could. "They were never interested in forming a real relationship with me, so I can't bring myself to think of them as my parents. Which they never actually were, because they didn't finalize the adoption.

"The media forgot about me and I started to get difficult, if you can imagine that," she halfheartedly joked, receiving a comforting squeeze for the effort. "So they relinquished their guardianship and gave me back to the state."

He finally spoke. "Holy— Rose, I—" He let out a harsh breath. "You gotta be kidding me."

"Hey, it's okay. Everything turned out. Dr. Williams kind of made me his pet project, trying to figure out what was up with my brain. He inspired me to become a doctor. I figured I could even take a shot at my own case. But I've since decided that some things are better left forgotten. Besides, I have Dylan now." Someone who needed her love as much as she needed to be loved unconditionally.

"So you're content not knowing?" he asked in an incredulous tone.

"Content?" She didn't know the meaning of the word, or at least she hadn't until she'd found herself in Brendan's arms. "As content as my nightmares will let me be."

"Don't you wonder if there might have been foul play involved? That you could have been—I don't know—kidnapped or something, and your family is still out there, wondering what happened to you?"

"Of course. That was my ultimate fantasy." Until she started to imagine a man like Brendan coming into her life and making it all not matter. "My picture was plastered all over the media for a while. Especially during the ratings sweeps, when one of the stations needed a boost. If anyone had been looking for me, they would have found me."

He grew silent. The rapid rise and fall of his chest beneath her hand made her realize he hadn't been breathing much at all before. "I'm sorry, Brendan. I know you assumed that my familiarity with charities came from the donor's side, not the receiving side."

"I—I would have never guessed, Rose. Hell, I remember thinking you must have been a debutante at some time."

"Now that's rich." She propped herself up to meet his gaze. "Look, hardly anyone remembers about this, and I'd like to keep it that way. It was bad enough having to muck around in it again with the adoption board over Dylan. Fortunately, they're legally bound—"

"You can trust me, Rose." The indignation was

clear in his tone, even if the dim light kept her from seeing it in his eyes.

She wanted to weep with joy. "I know. Which is why I told you. That and because I needed to." She dropped a tentative kiss on his lips. He kissed her back. Maybe this wasn't the last chapter in her fantasy come to life, after all. And if it was, she knew exactly how she wanted it to end.

Against his mouth she murmured, "It seems you stir all sorts of needs in me, Mr. MacDougal."

He made a growling noise deep in his throat and rolled her onto her back. Settling his heavenly weight on top of her, he kissed her deeply and thoroughly. His big body pressed her into the mattress and claimed her as his own, for the moment at least. She accepted his claim and opened to him, cradling him every way she could.

The almost desperate air to his passion made Rose fear he wasn't handling her news well. But if this was the last time she'd make love with Brendan, at least she'd have no regrets.

She hoped.

Chapter Thirteen

Brendan woke the next morning as stunned by Rose's revelation as he'd been when exhaustion finally claimed him near dawn. How could his assumptions about the beautiful woman in bed next to him have been so wrong? How could she be so different from him, yet fit into his world so effortlessly, and feel so right in his arms?

Most damning of all, after Rebecca, how could he have partnered with—hell, let himself become emotionally involved with—a woman he hardly knew? Her evasiveness should have made him jump ship right off instead of drawing him closer.

His judgment *was* questionable.

His insides churning, he slipped from her bed and went to shower in his own bathroom, needing to clear his head before he faced her again. They were supposed to fly back to Chicago first thing this morning, where she would return to work while he informed the hospital board of last night's fund-raising success.

Then what?

Brendan stepped beneath the shower spray, but his thinking only became more muddled. Should he walk away from her completely because he couldn't risk attaching his name to a woman who wasn't completely above reproach? A man in his position had to appear squeaky clean or everyone would distrust him, not just the Van Hovens of the world.

The thought of walking away from Rose for any reason made him feel sick to his stomach. If only he could close his eyes to what she'd told him. If only he didn't need to look back. But his need was too strong.

Was it not knowing what her past held that made it seem threatening?

At least there was a simple solution to not knowing. He doubted the resources and effort given to Rose's case twenty-five odd years ago could compare to what he would be able to muster now. It would take him all of one phone call to set in motion an investigation second to none. He'd uncover the truth of Rose's past as quickly as humanly possible.

And then?

Images of her gliding down the stairs the night before, a dream come true in the blue dress he'd bought her, heated him more than hot water could.

The memory of her in his arms, moving beneath him as he made love to her, made him hard again.

He turned the tap to cold and forced himself to focus on facts, not feeling. He knew in the pit of his gut now that it was emotion, not simple physical attraction, fueling the fire he had burning for Rose.

And he had to know the truth before he could comfortably label his feelings for her, whatever those labels turned out to be.

He clearly couldn't trust his judgment.

ROSE DIDN'T KNOW what to think. The way Brendan had made love to her after she'd told him about her past, or lack thereof, made her believe perhaps it wasn't over between them. But he was already up and showering when she awoke, and before she could muster the nerve to join him he'd dressed and poked his head into the room to tell her a continental breakfast was waiting for her. He had a few phone calls to make, and then they needed to get to the airport. The door to his suite of rooms closed with an ominous snap behind him.

No "How'd ya sleep, babe?" or anything.

Pain knifed through her heart. What had she done?

She'd taken too big a gamble by telling him her secret, that's what, and the consequences would be what they would be.

She drew a calming breath and sought to cauterize the wound in her heart and rein in her emotions with cool logic. She was jumping to conclusions. Insecurity was making her oversensitive and downright paranoid. Having kept her heart locked away for so long, she could chalk it up to inexperience.

Feeling much better, she showered in the luxurious cream marble bathroom adjacent to her room and dressed as quickly as she could. The only thing she took time with was placing the blue gown back into its garment bag. Last night, she'd draped it over a chair, where she could see it shimmering in the foyer light as she drifted off to sleep.

Some fantasies were harder to let go of, and last night she hadn't been quite ready to stop pretending she was a princess. Just as she wasn't prepared now to let go of the fantasy of a future with Brendan.

With her bags packed and waiting by the door near Brendan's, she wandered through the immensely livable suite, finally taking a seat at a small glass table next to a window with an incredible view of Central Park. It struck her yet again how different their pasts were, even though they currently shared so much common ground. Could they find a way to mesh their futures, also?

Only time, not to mention Brendan's behavior, would tell. Pushing aside her worries, she devoured a bowl of fruit and a bran muffin, having been too nervous to eat much at dinner the night before. One thing she *did* have experience with was worrying on an empty stomach, and she had no intention of making herself sick today.

Brendan returned to the suite just as she put the last oversize bite of muffin in her mouth. His face lit up with a knee-melting smile when he saw her. "Now there's a sight I like. A beautiful doctor having breakfast at my table."

Basking in his compliment and the hope it stirred, she dared to venture into the world of teasing. "Happen often, does it?" she said around the mouthful of muffin.

"If I have anything to say on the matter, it will."

Rose's heart convulsed. She forced the last bite down and returned his smile with a heartfelt one of her own. "I'll put out the word."

He started toward her, his movements sensually predatory. "I imagine there's some sort of club."

An elementary response triggered in her. Oh, how she wanted to be with him forever. Her skin prickled in anticipation the second he was close enough to touch her. "That's right. Beautiful Doctors Who Scarf Muffins."

He tortured her by planting his hands on the table and leaning close without making contact. "How about the Beautiful Doctor Muffin Scarfers? BDM Scarfers for short. I could have bumper stickers made."

She sat up straighter to bring her mouth closer to his. "One would look great on the limo."

He captured her mouth with his for a hot, toe-curling kiss, then pulled away enough to say, "Speaking of the limo, it's waiting out front. We need to get to the airport."

"Oh. Right." Though she didn't want this fantasy with Brendan to end, she was anxious to get back to Dylan.

As if on cue, a soft knock sounded on the door.

Brendan straightened away from her. "Come in."

The limousine driver entered and picked up their bags.

Brendan offered her his hand. It felt so natural and right to slip her fingers into his, and Rose allowed herself to savor the moment, expecting him to let go after she stood. He didn't. He held her hand the entire way downstairs, his grip gentle but firm. The simple act reassured her and settled her nerves in a way logic never could have.

Mary MacDougal was waiting at the base of the grand staircase, as beautiful in navy blue slacks and a simple cream blouse as she'd been in a formal gown. And she looked decidedly pleased as they descended the stairs hand in hand. Rose's throat tightened at the thought of having a loving mother figure like Mary in her life.

Yet another fantasy.

Mary spread her arms and reached for Rose the moment they stepped from the stairs. Brendan released her hand so she could accept his mother's hug.

Her embrace was firm and genuine. "I'm sorry you have to leave us so soon, Rose."

Rose's eyes burned with surprisingly strong regret. "So am I." She returned the hug, then stepped back. "But thank you very much for having me, and for all you've done for the hospital's fund-raiser."

"You're very welcome. Our family is fully aware of how blessed we are, and we try to take every opportunity to help." She looked to her son, her eyes shining with love. "I am so proud that Brendan has made our charities his life's work."

He pulled a face. "Yeah, well, I suck at it."

Mary reached for him. "Oh, Brendan." She stood on the tips of her toes and planted a firm kiss on his cheek. "What's past is past. And you're already doing the right thing again." She nodded significantly at Rose, making her blush.

He made a grunting sound that Rose took to be noncommittal, but his mother beamed as if it were a sign of agreement.

The driver came through the front door and held it open. It was time to leave. They finished their goodbyes, Mary saying how she looked forward to seeing Rose again.

Rose found herself hoping with all her being she would.

On the drive to the airport, where the MacDougal private jet awaited them, she couldn't stop thinking about what Mary had said about how blessed her family was. Rose's heart still ached over Brendan's frustration over his tarnished image.

On board the plane, Brendan chose the seat next to hers rather than the one facing her, as he had on the way to New York, and bolstered Rose's confidence. "I've been thinking about what your mother said this morning," she murmured.

He gave her a decidedly worried look. "Which part?"

"The part about how blessed your family is. I hope you see it, too."

He gestured at the plush interior of the private jet. "It's kind of hard to miss."

She gave him an exasperated grin. "I'm not talking about the money. I'm talking about the family. Take it from me, you're very blessed."

He gathered her hand in his and rubbed the back with his thumb. "I know, Rose. Don't think I take it for granted."

"Then why do you let the state of your reputation bother you so much?"

"Because my reputation is who I am."

"No it's not. What you do, and the reasons you do it, define who you are."

"But people's opinion of me is what allows me to do what I do. So I'm at the mercy of my reputation. They have to trust me before they'll give me their money."

Ashamed at how quick she'd been to distrust him

when they'd first met, and again when Bobby Ray had contacted her, she fell silent.

Brendan turned the tables on her. "How do you feel about *your* reputation?"

She rolled her eyes. "You mean the whole 'Dr. Doberman' thing?"

"Yeah, that thing."

She shrugged. "It allows me to be a pretty effective doctor, since the techs, nurses and other physicians know there's not much point arguing with me."

He raised his brows. "A woman used to getting her way."

Talk about the pot calling the kettle black. She returned the look. "You have a problem with that?"

"Not at all." He brought her hand to his lips for a quick kiss. "It's just a good thing I'm not too intimidated by Dobermans to get close to one."

She swallowed hard at his calling her on using her reputation to keep people at bay. And after everything she'd told him the night before, he knew exactly why.

Pulling their joined hands toward her mouth, she dropped a kiss on the back of *his* hand. "That's because, deep down, you know you're the type of man who can be trusted. Even by a Doberman."

He made the same noise in the back of his throat he had earlier, and pulled her toward him for a seemingly heartfelt kiss. She felt herself soaring in a way his private jet never could.

Her hopes soared, too. Perhaps the fantasy of her ideal man had indeed come true.

AFTER THEY REACHED the hospital later that morning, Brendan plucked Rose's heartstrings again when he asked to accompany her to see Dylan before he went on to tell Dr. Williams about their fund-raiser's success.

Rose received the best possible greeting from Dylan. He'd been napping, but when his groggy eyes spotted her next to his bed he sat up and reached for her with what sounded very much like "Mommy."

Rose gathered him into her arms and immediately burst into tears. It seemed her tough hide had been irreparably damaged by the two very important guys in her life. One she knew was now hers to keep. The other... Her gaze met Brendan's over Dylan's blond head. Well, the other might just have to be convinced.

Brendan reached into the breast pocket of his leather coat and produced a handkerchief like the one she'd wanted to shove down his throat the day she'd thought he'd betrayed her.

She laughed through her tears as she accepted it.

He shrugged. "I have several. They come in handy when my more sensitive patrons are overly touched by the needs of the children."

She gave him a chastising look for being so manipulative, but Dylan had made her too happy to care. "Did you hear him?"

His grin wide, Brendan came forward and ran a big hand over Dylan's hair. "I did."

She leaned back to look into the little boy's sweet face. "Can you do it again? Can you say Momma?"

Dylan looked her in the eye, grinned and made more noise than she'd ever heard from him. Granted, the faint sounds were incomprehensible, unlike what she could swear he'd said a moment ago, but his progress was monumental.

"Wow, sweetheart!" she exclaimed. His smile grew bigger. "Maybe all you needed was a little time and a whole lot of love. Let's go find Delores and Dr. Williams to see if this is something new, or if I've just been missing out." Rose glanced at Brendan as he followed her, half expecting to resent him a bit for enticing her away from Dylan for the New York fund-raiser, but the bitter emotion never came.

All she felt was the warmth of a shared miracle. He clearly cared about Dylan, too. Her heart threatened to burst with love at the thought of what a wonderful father Brendan would make, what a wonderful family the three of them would be.

The stunned look on Delores's face when Dylan answered Rose's prompt with more noises confirmed that Rose hadn't missed any precious moments. Brendan hadn't cost her a thing.

Except maybe the ability to protect her heart.

THE NEXT WEEK WENT BY IN A blur of happiness for Rose. Granted temporary guardianship of Dylan, she was able to discharge him from the hospital and bring him home. They were joined nearly every night by Brendan, who greeted her attempts at cooking dinner with studied aplomb. It didn't take Rose long to accept that Dylan was happiest eating macaroni and cheese that came from a box, canned fruit, and frozen chicken nuggets that only needed reheating.

Not wanting to confuse Dylan, she and Brendan had agreed it would be best if he didn't spend the night. But they had made out like a couple of teenagers on the couch more than once after Dylan was sound asleep.

As happy as she was, Rose couldn't shake the ominous feeling that a clock was ticking where she and Brendan were concerned. His penthouse in Chicago was leased; his life and real home were in New York. His time in Chicago had to be nearing an end. There had been no talk of the future.

Her concern prompted her to come up with a way she might convince him to stay in her life. She would offer her help with the one thing most important to him—restoring his reputation—by trying to make all his fund-raising efforts as successful as possible.

She made her decision as she was taking Dylan from the hospital play area, where he spent his days, to his speech therapy session. She kissed him on the head and asked, "What do you think, Dylan? Should we help Brendan?"

He babbled a happy string of *B* sounds.

"I'll take that as a yes. Who knows, maybe a national campaign with your cute little mug will generate enough donations to expand a whole bunch of pediatric programs."

Dylan tried out the *P* sound and made her laugh.

Her heart full of purpose, she left him with the therapist. She had just enough time to go to Brendan's penthouse, where he'd been working, and offer him their continued help.

He looked surprised but pleased to see her. "A nooner?" he asked, stepping aside and holding the door open for her.

"A what?" Then it dawned on her what he was hoping she had come for. While it would be heaven to make love to him on the spot, cold hardwood or not, Dylan's speech therapy wouldn't last that long. "Oh! No, sorry. No time for afternoon delight." But the fact he'd suggested it earned him a kiss.

He wrapped his arms around her tightly, deepening the kiss.

It was all Rose could do to end it. "No, really, Brendan. I have less than an hour." She pulled away. "Dylan's speech therapist can only hold his attention for that long."

"How's he doing?"

"He's making progress, but he still seems to

choose to not form words. Sometimes he responds to prompts, sometimes he doesn't.''

''But at least now you know that it's not because he can't.''

Thinking of her own inability to remember despite the absence of any apparent physical cause, she walked toward the long dining room table Brendan used as a desk. ''There are degrees of *can't*.''

''He'll get there, Rose. He knows he has your support.''

''Speaking of support—'' She started to turn toward him, but a large manila envelope on top of the balance sheets Brendan had been working on caught her eye. Or more specifically, the logo that served as the return address caught her eye, and raised the hairs on the back of her neck.

Morton Private Investigators.

Then in smaller print beneath the name: *Specializing in missing persons since 1979.*

The earth's motion seemed to slow as she picked up the envelope. It was addressed to Brendan, but hadn't been opened. The look on his face told her everything.

She asked anyway. ''Does this have anything to do with me?''

He pulled in a chest-expanding breath. ''Yes.''

All the old hurts from being the object of so many people's morbid curiosity throbbed like a pulsing bass. ''Why?''

''Because I have to know.''

Chapter Fourteen

Rose stared at Brendan, anger and blinding pain swelling with the destructive force of a storm off Lake Michigan. "You have to know? What do you mean, you *have to know?*"

He spread his arms wide, but there was very little supplication in his posture, only an air of helplessness. "I just do, Rose. Because of everything that happened with Rebecca."

"Rebecca? Rebecca Crest-whatever? The woman who scammed you?"

He dropped his hands and exhaled noisily. "Yes. Rebecca Crestfield."

Bewilderment joined Rose's growing sense of betrayal. "Are you saying that because I can't remember who I really am or where I came from, you're lumping me together with a crook?" She waved the envelope at him. "What did you think you'd find? That I was a hardened criminal at the age of six?"

He started to pace, heading toward the beautiful

view, which seemed to mock her growing misery. The frustration she'd sensed in him at the auction paled in comparison to what was rolling off him now. "No. You're nothing like Rebecca."

"But you just said—"

"I need to know everything about you." He stopped in front of the windows and buried his hands in the pockets of his chinos. "I can't afford any surprises in your background."

"Surprises? Like what? That I sprang from bad seed?"

He shot her a chastising glare.

A familiar pain started shoving its way in next to her anger. It seemed Dylan was the only person on earth who would ever truly love her for who she was in the here and now. "I told you everything, Brendan. You already know my secret. I trusted *you.*"

His chin dropped to his chest, but he still didn't look at her. "I know. But I trusted Rebecca without knowing anything about her. I let her into my life completely. Into my heart."

Rose's own heart jolted and a surprising white-hot jealousy grabbed hold of her insides. After all he'd done, she could still be jealous over him. She shook her head in despair that she was so pitiful.

He pulled his hands from his pockets and turned to face her, a deep misery darkening his hazel eyes. "I swore to myself that I would never trust another woman in that way, unless I knew everything about her and she met certain…requirements." He had the grace to look ashamed after using such a word. "I need to know that your past is as above reproach as your present."

He pointed at the envelope in her hand and came toward her. "If that report proves my theory correct, that you were kidnapped rather than abandoned, then…"

"Then what? I'll be more acceptable?"

He looked stricken. "No. That's not what I mean—"

"Then what do you mean? You said it, so you're going to have to explain yourself."

He made a frustrated sound and looked at the ceiling. "Rose, you're twisting this around—"

"No! No I'm not." What she was doing was teetering on the brink of hysteria. "You wanted to prove I was kidnapped to make yourself feel better, to make me seem okay in your eyes. But do you really think I'll be less fodder for the tabloids? I have news for you, Brendan, the tale of Little Lost Rose generated plenty of press when everyone assumed I'd been abandoned. Trust me, finding out that I'd been kidnapped would *not* prove less damaging to your reputation."

The mere threat of this kind of pain had kept her alone most of her life. It clogged her throat and brought tears to her eyes.

She couldn't stop explaining now, though. He had to understand. She couldn't deal with the pain if he didn't understand.

She forced out, "That's why I told you the truth. If the media starts poking around into who I am, they are going to find a whole bunch of juicy stuff. I wanted you to know that. So you wouldn't be caught off guard if it happened. So you could make the choice."

Swallowing hard, she held her ground. "If you don't want to take the risk of being involved with me, fine. I knew I was taking a chance." Though she'd woefully underestimated the cost. "But to go behind my back to find out what I specifically said I didn't want to know…" She shook her head, fighting the burning moisture blurring her vision.

He reached for her. "The information in there might not be bad, Rose."

She stepped away. If he touched her, she'd shatter for sure. "But it could be *horrific*. Can't you see that? Something happened to me that my mind has chosen to completely erase."

She spread her arms wide. "Why do you think I went into pediatric neurology? I wanted to understand what had happened to me, and offer that understanding to my patients." She let her hands drop heavily to her sides, weighted down by a sense of defeat. "But I've discovered that sometimes we're not meant to understand, and I've accepted that I am who I am.''

Tears won the battle and streamed down her face. ''Okay, I lied. It's not fine that you don't want to be involved with me. Do you have any idea what it feels like to know that I'm not good enough as I am for you to care about me?'' She ached for the loss of the man who had joked with her, held her in his arms, made her feel safe.

''Rose...'' He reached for her again, his expression full of pity.

The look snapped her out of her downward spiral. She'd been pitied enough in her life. She'd also been a victim of her past for far too long. As had Brendan. He was making choices based on what had happened to him in the past.

She narrowed her eyes. ''You know what, Brendan? I think that you're only willing to commit to a woman who's above reproach because you're afraid to take the risk of loving the wrong woman. You trusted a thief, so you doubt your own judgment too much.''

Her heart withering, she tossed the envelope onto the table. She needed to finish this once and for all. ''Even if what's in that report somehow makes me acceptable in your life, I can't open it. And I don't want to know what it contains. As much as I want to be with you—'' Her voice broke, and she had to pull in a deep, shuddering breath before she could continue. "I can't take the risk that it holds something else. Some things are best left forgotten, Brendan."

"I didn't intend to hurt you, Rose."

His apology was a puny bandage on a major wound. Awash with a hurt that burned clear to her core, she straightened her shoulders and sought refuge in the tough, thorny persona that had protected her for so many years. The once-hard shell that Brendan and his charm had somehow managed to crack and sneak through.

"But you did hurt me, and I let you. I should have known fantasies don't come true."

Never in her life had it hurt so much to walk away from someone, but she had no choice. He would never love her the way she needed him to: unconditionally. Rose turned on her heel and left the penthouse, taking what was left of her heart.

She needed to get back to the hospital, to her sanctuary. There, with Dylan, she'd try to stuff the agonizing hurt and disappointment into the dark corner inside her where she kept the rest of her baggage.

She tried to shut out all thoughts on the way back to the hospital, but images of Brendan's smile, memories of his touch and his smooth, sensual voice in the night wouldn't be completely banished. Once she reached the hospital she was hit by a longing for his kiss, a yearning for his comfort. But she successfully squelched her need—until she passed a huge bouquet of roses waiting to be delivered to a patient. Brendan had the gall to haunt her in the pediatric wing's corridors.

She paused outside the speech therapist's office long enough to completely calm her breathing and clear her eyes of any trace of tears. She prayed Dylan wouldn't wonder why the big man with the ready smile no longer joined them for macaroni and cheese and canned peaches.

She cringed inwardly at how easily, how fully she'd let Brendan into her life and Dylan's. She should never have allowed him near her little boy. No fantasy was worth Dylan's sense of security.

Forcefully unclenching her jaw, Rose stepped into the brightly decorated office used by the linguistic specialists. Dylan was sitting on the multicolored, interlocking block mats, playing with sock puppets with Dr. Jan Sothern.

Rose smiled when Dylan's puppet, which was on his hand sideways, gave Jan's puppet a big, smacking kiss rather than answer a question about his name. The ache throbbing inside her receded slightly. He really was a balm to her wounds.

She normally wouldn't have intruded on a session, but she desperately needed a hug. She took a few steps toward them and Dylan looked her way. The smile that lit up his face brought tears to her eyes again. He scrambled to his feet and ran to her.

Dropping to her knees, she opened her arms and he barreled into her with a three-year-old's enthusiasm.

Rose hugged him tightly. "Oh, my sweet, sweet boy."

His little arms wrapped around her neck and he squeezed back. "Love you." His words were as clear and as plain as day.

Shock sent her back on her heels. Jan's wide-eyed, openmouthed expression confirmed that Rose hadn't imagined what she'd heard, that her desperate need for unconditional love hadn't manufactured his words in her head.

She pulled back to see his face. "Dylan, I heard your words! You said them so well!"

Her praise made him glow.

Touching her nose to his, she poured every tattered shard of her heart into what she said. "And I love you, too. Very, very much."

He rewarded her with a kiss on the cheek from his crooked hand puppet.

Rose laughed through her tears and hugged him again.

Jan said, "Wow. He's been mouthing words, but I hadn't been able to get him to actually vocalize. He's apparently just selective about who he talks to." She laughed and held up a hand. "But that's okay, as long as he's talking."

More likely Dylan had decided the awful things

he'd experienced in his short existence weren't bad enough to keep him from moving forward with his life. How could one so small and so vulnerable be so resilient?

Rose envied him.

The idea of putting the past behind her once and for all sounded so wonderful. The chance to move forward with her own life, to have the future she only dared imagine in her dreams. She was tired to the bottom of her soul of pretending she didn't need anyone. Dylan had blown that farce clean out of the water.

So had Brendan.

If only she were brave enough to face what she needed to learn about her past to move on, to be happy.

Because for starters what would make her happy would be a family of her very own, made up of Brendan and Dylan. Her heart wrenched at the thought that it would never happen. But since she'd spent her life not going along for the ride for fear of being abandoned yet again, how could she expect to be anywhere but left behind? Could she risk a relationship, even if she mustered the courage to read Brendan's private investigator's report?

The notion of stepping out onto that crumbling ledge was so frightening, so new.

She looked at Jan. ''Is it all right if I take Dylan

to Dr. Williams and tell him about—or hopefully, show him—our little breakthrough?''

Jan wiped a tear from her own eye. "Definitely. Go ahead. But I would like to spend a bit more time with Dylan afterward. It would be great to catch him speaking on video for his file.''

"No problem. I'll bring him right back." Rose released Dylan and encouraged him back far enough that she could get to her feet, then hoisted him up with a grunt and settled him on her hip. While small for his age from lack of proper nutrition and care, he still was a load, but Rose wasn't inclined to let him out of her arms yet.

Not caring if anyone noticed the streaks tears had left on her face—tears of joy—Rose carried Dylan to Dr. Williams's office. They found him working at his desk.

"Do you have a minute?" she asked.

Her mentor smiled. "Sure, come on in." His gaze traveled over her face and the smile faded. He stood and rounded the desk. "What's wrong?"

"Nothing." It was a lie, but an appropriate one at the moment. "We've had a very, very happy thing happen just now, haven't we, Dylan?"

The stinker gave her a bland look. She prayed his decision to speak wouldn't turn out to be a one-time event.

She readjusted him on her hip and whispered, "Say 'love you.'"

He buried his face against her neck.

Knowing she'd been pushing her luck trying to get him to perform on command, she kissed his head and looked back at Dr. Williams. "When I came to pick him up from Jan Sothern's office he very clearly said 'love you' to me. Jan heard him, too."

Dr. Williams's gray eyebrows shot up. "He spoke? Actual words?"

She nodded, tears welling in her eyes again. "Actual, *meaningful* words."

"That's wonderful!" He patted Dylan's back. "Good job, Dylan! I'm so proud of you." To Rose he said, "I guess all he needed was time and love."

Rose snuggled against Dylan's silky head. Was that why she'd never healed? Because while she'd had plenty of time, she hadn't been given—then didn't allow—the kind of love she needed?

But now she had Dylan in her life. If she'd been willing to discover what had happened to her before she'd been found under a rosebush, she might have had Brendan, too.

Assuming, of course, the report held what he needed it to for her to be in his life. And even if it didn't, could she convince him to give her a chance, anyway? Could she make him see that no matter what her past held, his judgment was sound, and his decision to trust her had been the right one? That his heart would be safe with her?

Would she be able to heal then?

And she wasn't the only victim of the past. Brendan was making choices, clinging to expectations, because of what had happened to him before. He was making mistakes, just as she had. Judging from the look on his face when she'd walked away, he was suffering from them, too.

One thing she knew for sure—she'd be happier than she'd ever been in her life if she could convince him. Wasn't that alone worth the risk?

Maybe it wasn't too late for her and Brendan. Rose's chest filled with an empowering sense of purpose that threatened to burst her if she didn't act.

She met Dr. Williams's kind gaze. "Do you have a meeting you might be on your way to soon?"

He moved to his desk and touched the screen of his electronic planner. "Nothing until a dinner meeting at six."

"Would you be willing to do me a favor? One that involves this guy?" She jiggled Dylan, making him laugh.

Dr. Williams eyed her for a minute, probably wondering how much further she expected him to stretch hospital policy.

She rushed to explain, "I only need you to take Dylan back down to Jan's office—she wanted to see if she could get him to speak on video—and ask her to take him to the day care if I'm not back by the time she's done."

Dr. Williams grinned and reached for Dylan, who

obliged by practically jumping from Rose's arms into his. "Well, heck, that's an easy one. I can certainly manage that."

"Great. Thank you very much."

His gaze turned speculative. "Important business?"

She filled her lungs and squared her shoulders. "I'm going to go see a man about the future."

He raised both gray brows for the second time.

She grinned and stepped close to give Dylan a kiss. "You have fun playing with Dr. Jan again, sweetheart. I won't be gone long. Love you," she said, and turned to leave.

Dylan's high, scratchy voice echoed, "Love you," stopping her in her tracks.

"Hey," Dr. Williams exclaimed in delight, leaning back to get a better look at the child in his arms. "That was wonderful, Dylan! Good boy!"

Rose hurried to them and gave Dylan more kisses and praise. "See? Doesn't he say it well?"

Dr. Williams nodded. "Very well. And clearly. I think we've definitely turned a corner with this one."

Rose agreed and headed for the door again. She paused long enough to blow Dylan one last kiss.

He waved and pronounced, "Love you," yet again.

Tears blurred Rose's vision as she left the office.

She hoped it wasn't too late to garner the same sort of declaration from one Brendan Logan MacDougal.

And that she was strong enough to handle what his private investigator had discovered about her. Dylan had shown her that without facing the past, without daring to look her demons in the eye, she'd never be able to heal and build a happy future.

BRENDAN HAD NEVER realized misery could be so suffocating. He retraced the path he was wearing between the penthouse's floor-to-ceiling windows and the dining room table, driven by the memory of the pain in Rose's voice.

And the truth in her words.

I think that you're only willing to commit to a woman who's above reproach because you're afraid to take the risk of loving the wrong woman. You trusted a thief, so you doubt your own judgment too much.

He glanced away from the rain-spattered window and the dreary, overcast view of a weather system that had blown in to match his mood. He had no choice but to admit Rose was right. His need to know the truth about her past—a truth that consisted of really nothing more than the potentially ugly reason she had been abandoned unconscious in a city park—was misguided.

She didn't have to have a "respectable" background for him to trust her enough to love her.

Because he already loved her.

The agony that had seared his chest when he'd made her cry—and leave—confirmed his feelings. How could he have been so stupid? So stubborn? So blinded by the consequences of the idiotic choices he'd made in the past?

Rose wasn't a woman out to hurt him or use him. She was a woman who deserved to be loved and cherished.

And trusted.

God help him if he couldn't think of a way to convince her to forgive him.

He looked at the unopened manila envelope containing the private investigator's report on the table. The first step he needed to take was to eliminate the evidence of his misplaced distrust, both symbolically and physically.

He snatched up the envelope and headed for the kitchen. He had to dig through a few drawers, but finally found a long-barreled butane lighter. He hauled the heavy plastic garbage can from beneath the sink, held the envelope over it and pulled the lighter's trigger. A flame ignited with a click.

If Rose didn't want to face what her past might hold, then he sure as hell wouldn't make her. Because it wouldn't change the woman she was now.

Hopefully, burning the investigator's report to ashes would be enough to prove his trust.

Prove that he loved her no matter what her past held, because he couldn't imagine life without her.

Chapter Fifteen

Rose knocked hard on the door to Brendan's penthouse, gripped by an urgency akin to what she felt when a child's life was on the line. Only it was her own life, her own future at stake.

Brendan's gruff voice sounded from somewhere within the apartment. "Just a damn minute."

Something in his tone made the hairs on the back of her neck stand on end for the second time that day. He sounded in pain. She tried the knob and pushed, surprised when the door opened. He hadn't locked it after she'd stormed out. She slipped inside, scanning the large living area for Brendan as she shut the door behind her.

She was about to announce herself when the acrid smell of something burning led her to the kitchen. She froze in her tracks at the sight of Brendan holding the manila envelope over a garbage can, a butane lighter at one corner. The envelope was turning black and starting to curl as the flame danced beneath it.

"Brendan! No!" she cried, lunging toward him. Startled, he stood motionless as she snatched the envelope from his grasp, stuck it in the sink and grabbed the faucet. Though her shaking hands made it difficult, she tried to wet only the burning edge.

"Rose, what are you doing? Why are you back?" Surprise had replaced the pain in his voice.

She made sure the corner of the envelope, and the papers it contained, were no longer glowing red before she turned around. Her pounding heart stuttered at the look in Brendan's hazel eyes. There was surprise, all right, but also anguish and regret.

Maybe she wasn't taking such a risk coming here, after all. Her hopes skyrocketed.

He frowned fiercely. "Why did you do that?"

She raised her chin and willed her pulse to slow down. "So I can read it. Which would have been difficult if you'd burned it to a crisp."

He shook his head. "No. I hurt you by asking for the report. You didn't deserve to have your wishes ignored."

Her growing hope elbowed for space among the emotions in her crowded chest. She retrieved the envelope from the sink. "Someone who is braver than I am showed me it's time to put the hurt to rest."

"You shouldn't have been hurt in the first place.

You were right. I shouldn't have hired a P.I. firm to dig around. It wasn't my business, and my reasons for doing it were screwed up. You helped me realize that. I was an idiot.''

Her heart started pounding again, only this time from dread. ''Because you can't be with me, anyway?''

He shook his head. ''Because what happened to me in the past made me stupid.'' He snagged the report from her hand, catching her off guard.

She grabbed for it, but he held it out of her reach. The garbage can between them kept her from jumping for it.

He gave her an annoyed look. ''And because I don't need to know everything to trust you. I already trust you.''

Trust didn't equal love. She still had to face her demons to be able to love him the way he deserved.

She pointed at the envelope. ''I've decided I'm ready to face what's in there, Brendan. Even if what I've feared for so many years—that I was abused— turns out to be true. Because then I'll know what sort of help to get. And be able to move forward with my life.''

She drew in a shaky breath and took the plunge. ''Hopefully with you.''

He lowered the envelope, his hazel eyes intent on her face. ''What are you saying?''

''I'm saying I'm willing to do anything, deal with

anything, to have you in my life. To fight for the chance to win your love.''

A smile slowly spread across his face and he snorted. ''Now that's ironic, because you already have it.''

Rose's world tilted. She saved herself from falling by reaching back and grabbing the edge of the sink behind her. She hadn't seen it coming. Not at all. The thought that a man like Brendan already loved a woman like her, a woman who'd kept secrets and had done everything she could to keep everyone at arm's length, was unbelievable.

He gave a wry shake of his head. ''It finally dawned on me after you left that the past can't change the woman you are now, just as my reputation doesn't define who I am.''

His gaze softened as it traveled over her face. ''And I've fallen in love with the woman you are, Rose. I don't need to know anything else about you. I also don't want to see you hurt anymore.'' He ignited the butane lighter with a loud click and relit the envelope.

''Brendan!'' Unswayed, Rose leaped for it once more, knocking over the garbage can with a thud on the glossy hardwood floor. She snatched the report back before he could jerk it away. He'd lit a bottom corner that had stayed dry during the first dousing and wasn't as thick as the top flap corner, so the flame flared easily.

Fortunately, a puddle of water had remained in the sink, and Rose dropped the burning part of the envelope directly into it. The fire sputtered out without so much as a hiss.

Brendan stepped close behind her and his big hands covered her shoulders. "Please, Rose. Don't do it for me. I don't need to know. I swear."

"But I do. I need to put my demons to rest once and for all. And I can't do that until I face them. Until I see what they are."

She stared at the envelope, but saw her life. The couple who had taken her into their lives, only to shut her out. The disconnectedness, the loneliness, the yearning, the nightmares. And all the people who would have loved her if she had let them. She'd been too afraid.

She shifted her gaze to his. "Ultimately, it's always been not knowing that was the worst. That's what has held me where I am. Unable to go forward or back." She pulled in a deep, fortifying breath. "I'm tired of living that way. You and Dylan showed me how wonderful my future could be, and dammit, I want it. Free and clear. With you."

Brendan's heart swelled to painful proportions in his chest. He couldn't believe this was really happening between them, that she had laid out a battle plan to win his love. Her willingness to face her worst fears about her past so she could have a future with him rocked him to his very soul.

And humbled him.

"I don't deserve you, Rose."

She was silent for a while, her shoulders rigid beneath his hands. Then she whispered, "The question is, do you want me?"

He nuzzled her hair, amazed at the step he found himself not just wanting, but needing to take with this woman. "I want you in a whole bunch of different ways, Doctor. But most of all, I want you happy."

She leaned into him, her head dropping back against his shoulder, and allowed him to support her. He held her close, anchoring her to him with one arm across her upper chest and the other around her slender waist. He could feel her heart pounding beneath his forearm, her ribs rising and falling with rapid, shallow breaths.

His strong, tenacious Dr. Doberman was scared.

The need to protect her, to ease her fear, caused every muscle in his body to contract. He tightened his grip, hugging her to him. He had never in his life felt this physical, primal drive to shelter a woman from harm. The fact that the harm would be emotional made him want to protect her more.

But after only a moment she straightened, pulling away from him so her back no longer touched his chest, squaring her shoulders in a fortifying move that touched his heart. And made him love her all the more.

"Okay. Time to do this."

Brendan took a final shot at talking her out of heading down the path of discovery he'd unfairly shoved her onto. "Rose—"

She stopped him with a sharply raised hand. "No, Brendan. If I don't look inside this envelope I'll never know true peace. And I'll hate myself for being a coward. It's bad enough that I ran from love all these years."

Not liking the thought of her settled down and happily married to some other guy long before he'd had the chance to meet her, he grumbled, "Maybe that has more to do with the fact that you hadn't met the right man yet."

Rose looked over her shoulder at Brendan and put her heart into her grin. How could he fill her with such love and happiness at such a terrifying moment? Because he *was* the right man for her. "You think I finally have?" she teased.

He closed the inch of space she'd created between them in her attempt to be strong. "Damn straight."

His declaration restored the determination that had brought her here in the first place, and she returned her attention to the sorry-looking manila envelope in the stainless steel sink. Her hand didn't shake this time when she reached to pick it up, choosing her future with Brendan over the ghosts in her past once and for all.

What had been Brendan's name and address was

now a wet smear of black ink, and the private investigation firm's return label had been mostly burned away. Rose took advantage of the blackened hole in the corner, sticking her finger into it and ripping the top open. The wet paper inside was stuck in place, so rather that pulling the report out she ripped the front of the envelope away.

The report must have been printed on a laser printer—none of the words had smeared, and it was all perfectly legible. A sign if she'd ever seen one.

Knowing Brendan would read over her shoulder, Rose moved out of his embrace. The stubborn pride that had allowed her to make it this far in life insisted she take this important step alone. She held the damp, black-edged papers before her.

"Wait." Brendan took a quick step toward her and brought her hands together, crushing the report between her fists. "Before you read that, I want to do something first."

"Brendan—"

"I don't want you to think that what I'm about to do was in any way influenced by what we're about to find out. I want you to be certain that it's because I love *you*. Who you are right at this moment, not who you might turn out to be."

He smiled that wicked, charming smile that had made her doubt her sanity when he'd first stepped from the shadows into her life. "If you turn out to be some long-lost heiress, I don't want you thinking I'm only after your money."

Rose gave a short, bewildered laugh. "Oh, yeah, because you really need more money."

"What I need is you, Rose." His expression sobered and he dropped down on one knee, her hands—and the crumpled report—held tightly in his.

It was all Rose could do to keep from going down on her knees with him. Only telling herself she was mistaken about what he was doing kept her standing.

With his hazel eyes warmed to caramel, he gazed up at her in a way that made her forget how to breathe. "Will you allow me to be a part of your future? As your husband and Dylan's father?"

When she simply stared at him in stunned disbelief, he implored, "Will you marry me, Rose?"

The only coherent thought in her haze of happiness was that she didn't want him to be making a mistake. "First, don't you want to know—"

He squeezed her hands. "I already told you I don't want to know what the report says. Now I'm proving it. My uncle was dead-on when he said you're Mrs. MacDougal material." He pulled her hands to his mouth for a kiss. "That's all that matters."

Mrs. Brendan MacDougal material.

Her eyes overflowed with tears as her heart overflowed with love. Rose corrected, "Mrs. Brendan *Logan* MacDougal. Mrs. BLM." She started to laugh silently through her tears. "I want a handkerchief with that embroidered on it."

He grinned. "You got it, sweetheart. So I can take that as a yes?"

Smiling as best she could with a trembling lower lip, Rose nodded. "Yes. I'll marry you."

He bolted up and released her hands to capture her face, giving her the most poignant, heartfelt kiss of her life. He then crushed her in his embrace, holding her to him as if he never intended to let her go.

Rose prayed he never would. "I love you, Brendan."

"I love you, Rose."

The smell of burned paper from the pages trapped between them brought her back to earth, or at least as close as she'd get with Brendan's love keeping her afloat.

She looked up at him. "I still need to read what your P.I. found out."

His chest expanded against her, reminding her of the size and strength that would forever be hers to lean on. He sighed so hard it ruffled her hair. "All right." He released her and stepped back. "But first..." He took off his gold class ring. "Let me see if this will fit you."

He held her left hand in his and slipped the ring onto her ring finger.

She gave him a questioning look, and he shrugged.

"It's just for now, so you'll know my proposal was for real."

While far from the right size, the flat-topped insignia ring wouldn't fall off too easily. She intended to keep her hand closed, just in case.

With her fantasies coming true right and left, Rose was having trouble feeling anything but surreal. Her throat too tight to speak, she went up on her toes and gave him a poignant kiss. When his arms came around her to prolong the moment, she took a quick step back and let him know with a look that she wouldn't be distracted.

He crossed his arms over his chest and muttered, "Fine."

Tapping into all the power and strength his love gave her, Rose shifted her attention to the papers in her left hand, and the glint of Brendan's ring brought tears of joy back to her eyes. She wiped them away. "Oh, I get it. You gave this ring to me so I wouldn't be able to read through my tears."

"As long as they're tears of happiness, I won't be sorry."

She blinked and forced herself to focus. As she read the report, her heart slowed to a steady, even rhythm, and an acceptance unlike anything she'd felt before centered her. She read it through a second time, to be certain she hadn't missed a detail— which she hadn't—then held the report out to Brendan.

He just looked at her.

"Take it. Please. I need you to read it."

He lowered his chin. "Just as long as we're square that *I* don't need to read it."

Love for him pulsing through her, she smiled softly. "We're square."

He took the wet, singed papers from her and began to read. When he reached the end, the look of love and understanding he gave her sent the tears rolling down her cheeks again.

Judging from the invoice attached to the report, Brendan had committed a king's ransom to the endeavor. But his cream-of-the-crop investigators had found the same thing as those who'd investigated her abandonment years ago.

Nothing.

She was still simply Rose Doeber.

A woman of her own making. A woman who had a future, even without having a past.

And the tears she cried were tears of joy. Because now she was so much more.

She was not only the mother of a beautiful little boy who trusted her with his love, she was also officially Mrs. MacDougal material.

They'd both met their match.

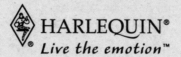

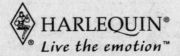

If you enjoyed what you just read,
then we've got an offer you can't resist!

Take 2 bestselling love stories FREE!

Plus get a FREE surprise gift!

///////////////////////////

Clip this page and mail it to Harlequin Reader Service®

IN U.S.A.	IN CANADA
3010 Walden Ave.	P.O. Box 609
P.O. Box 1867	Fort Erie, Ontario
Buffalo, N.Y. 14240-1867	L2A 5X3

YES! Please send me 2 free Harlequin American Romance® novels and my free surprise gift. After receiving them, if I don't wish to receive anymore, I can return the shipping statement marked cancel. If I don't cancel, I will receive 4 brand-new novels every month, before they're available in stores! In the U.S.A., bill me at the bargain price of $3.99 plus 25¢ shipping & handling per book and applicable sales tax, if any*. In Canada, bill me at the bargain price of $4.74 plus 25¢ shipping & handling per book and applicable taxes**. That's the complete price and a savings of at least 10% off the cover prices—what a great deal! I understand that accepting the 2 free books and gift places me under no obligation ever to buy any books. I can always return a shipment and cancel at any time. Even if I never buy another book from Harlequin, the 2 free books and gift are mine to keep forever.

154 HDN DNT7
354 HDN DNT9

Name _____ (PLEASE PRINT)

Address _____ Apt.# _____

City _____ State/Prov. _____ Zip/Postal Code _____

* Terms and prices subject to change without notice. Sales tax applicable in N.Y.
** Canadian residents will be charged applicable provincial taxes and GST.
  All orders subject to approval. Offer limited to one per household and not valid to
  current Harlequin American Romance® subscribers.
  ® are registered trademarks of Harlequin Enterprises Limited.

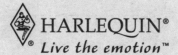

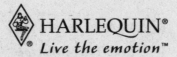